# THE
# QUEEN'S
# ANGEL

For information contact :
www.deerwoodpress.com

Book and Cover design by Lynn Harrod
Photos by Connor Botts, Daniel Gregoire, and Erik McLean
Edited by William McCoy

ISBN: 978-1-7367234-8-7 (ePub edition)
ISBN: 978-1-7367234-7-0 (Paperback edition)

First Edition: June 2022

# THE QUEEN'S ANGEL

*a novel*

## LYNN HARROD

*To my Father, whose faith was lost and found again,*
*each time surrounded by those who loved him.*

# 1

## One Day

Mornings on the streets of La Figueira during the summer months are not for the faint of heart. By nine o'clock, temperatures often hit the nineties. By noon, folks are trudging through triple digits with a thick, smoggy humidity. A quarter-million citizens called "La Fig" their home, nearly all of them miserable in the relentless heat.

The St. Nelia District, named for the historic church at its center, ran along the eastern outskirts of the city. The decayed urban neighborhood comprised twenty-eight blocks of mixed-use retail, low-income housing, freeway on-ramps, railroads, electrical towers, liquor stores, and hole-in-the-wall eateries of every ethnicity, all covered with five barrios worth of graffiti.

In the upper east side of the district stood the Royal Queen Motel, a fifteen-room relic from the 1950s. A long-shuttered pizza parlor boasting of a "fully air-conditioned dining room" and once-brilliant neon sign of a queen holding up a giant star were the only remnants of the motel's glory days. Gangs, homeless denizens, streetwalkers, and drug dealers replaced the traveling families that used to stop there on their way to the coast. Arrowhead Avenue, the main thoroughfare that once fed the motel a steady stream of tourists, was now derelict, lined with unending pavement cracks, potholes, and barbed wire.

Maria and Eduardo Ramirez, an elderly Mexican couple dressed in their Sunday best, stepped off a city bus and walked across the motel's weed-strewn parking lot to the manager's office. The only car in the lot was a lowrider, a dinged, faded silver 1960 Chevrolet Impala that used to be a sweet show car but had been long since neglected by its owner. Car clubs and auto shows are no longer on the calendar when living check-to-check.

Maria rested on the front bumper of the lowrider while her husband approached the office's walk-up window. Eduardo spotted the surly manager and tapped on the glass.

Carlos Cruz sat inside, a Latino-Filipino covered with tattoos, wearing a clean, white tank top, overpriced studio-quality headphones, and a permanent scowl. He zoned out to classic British heavy metal - his guilty pleasure - while reading a car magazine, never looking up from its pages.

Eduardo adjusted his fedora only to remove it respectfully as he pushed forth the introduction he had long dreaded. "I am Eduardo Ramirez," he said in Spanish. "This is my wife, Maria. Good morning, sir."

Carlos eyed the old woman sitting on his Impala's front bumper. It annoyed him to see someone treat his ride like a bench, but he let it go. He returned to his magazine.

"Is he here today?" Eduardo asked. "I was told he'd be here."

"Who?" Carlos asked in Spanish, not taking his eyes off his magazine.

"The Angel."

"Who?" Carlos laughed, feigning ignorance.

"Please, sir, where is he?" Desperate, Eduardo slid a fifty-dollar bill across the window counter. Carlos promptly swiped the money and stepped outside.

Intimidating, lean, and muscular out in the sun, the towering stone-faced Carlos looked like a gangster in his tight tank top and baggy pants. He gestured for the old couple to follow him to a nearby room. Eduardo guided his confused wife.

"Don't negotiate," Carlos ordered, continuing their Spanish. "Don't mention money at all. It offends him."

They walked down a corridor of peeling paint and crumbling stucco to Room 9. Carlos knocked and opened the door at the same time. He remained at the doorway like a guard as the elderly couple entered. Eduardo stepped onto the flattened, stained shag carpet and looked around the room, a simple suite in wildly outdated decor that would have been all the rage in the early 1970s. He gestured for Maria to sit in a chair as he turned to face the man he'd been so anxious to meet.

Abel Grant, a middle-aged African-American man in pressed jeans, a button-up shirt, and horn-rimmed eyeglasses entered from another room. He smoked a cigarette - as he constantly did - and spoke in a tone of business and control. He offered Eduardo a handshake.

"My name is Abel Grant."

Eduardo shook Abel's hand and struggled to speak English. "Mr. Grant... do remember... me? From St. Nelia church? Eduardo Ramirez. Please... do remember..."

"I remember you, Mr. Ramirez."

"Good," Eduardo smiled. "My wife... she Maria... she..."

Abel held up his hand, silencing the old man. "Did you pay Carlos?" Both the mention of money and the use of English confused Eduardo. "Did you pay this man?" Abel asked again, switching to rough Spanish.

"Yes," Eduardo said, relieved that the "angel" spoke his language.

"How much?"

"Fifty dollars. I'm sorry, it is all I have. But I can get more!"

Abel snuffed his cigarette in an ashtray on the bedside table and approached Carlos at the door. The giant gangster promptly handed over the cash. Abel leaned in close, staring down his imposing comrade. "If you take money from anyone ever again," Abel said in English, "we're done, and I will give back what I took from you nine years ago."

To Eduardo's surprise, Carlos couldn't look Abel in the eye. Instead, he bowed his head in shame as Abel returned the cash to the old man. He gestured for Maria to sit on the bed. Ever more confused, his money back in hand, Eduardo did as he was told.

"Tell me," Abel said in Spanish.

"Forty years ago, we came to America together," Eduardo began. "Forty years of marriage, six children, many grandchildren, and now my love doesn't know my face." He held back tears. "She's lost to me! I don't know what to do! Our children have all moved away. All we have now is each other, just like in the beginning."

"How long?"

"A year," the old man said. "A very hard year. Doctor says she will only get worse."

"You understand she may be beyond my help?"

Eduardo nodded, tried not to cry. Maria was oblivious, dazed, as Abel gripped her hand, lifting her face so they were eye-to-eye.

"So pretty in your Sunday dress," Abel said. Maria looked at him, unsure, afraid. "Don't be scared, Maria. I'm going to do my best to take it all away." Though she was hesitant, as if caught in a storm of emotion, Maria nodded "yes."

Abel held her hand a few different ways until he finally got *the feeling*. He shut his eyes and clasped his fingers with hers. The feeling grew stronger. Abel fell to one knee. Eduardo moved to help, but Carlos stopped him.

Abel breathed heavily, as if a weight had been placed on him. Maria slowly turned and looked about the room. She locked eyes with her husband. Eduardo could see his beloved wife returning.

Abel finally released her hand, remaining on one knee. Maria approached Eduardo. Husband and wife embraced as if for the first time. Abel rose to his feet, exhausted. "How do you feel, Maria?"

"I feel... light," Maria said in Spanish.

"What's your name, my love?" Eduardo asked. "Do you know who I am? Do you know..." Abel gestured for Eduardo to calm down, to give her a moment.

"I do know," Maria muttered. "I'm so sorry, Eduardo."

"It's not your fault." Eduardo's attempt at a strong front fell away as tears streamed down his face.

At the door, Carlos looked away, failing to hide his own emotions.

"It's a miracle!" Eduardo said. "A miracle! God is good! I thank God!" He turned to his savior, beaming with a smile he hadn't felt for ages. "I prayed day and night, and God brought me to you! His angel!"

Abel was unmoved. "The city bus brought you to me." He took off his glasses and pinched the bridge of his nose, trying to quell a headache as he readied a new cigarette from his pack of White Knights. He spoke his rough Spanish slowly, pointedly. "What God did was make her sick to begin with. You can thank Him for that."

"Yes," the old man recalled. "I was told you are angry with God. Reverend Dean says you don't need to believe to be under His watch. I know He was here today. I know you are His angel. And I thank you."

Eduardo took out the fifty-dollar bill from his coat pocket again and tried to place it in Abel's hand, but he refused. "The reverend told me you need payment," Eduardo said, again confused.

"Do you make anything for a living?" Abel asked. Eduardo shook his head. "Do you grow anything? Do you cook?"

"Maria bakes!" Eduard said. "My love is the best! Anything you want! Cakes! Pies!"

"Bake me a pie."

Eduardo quickly agreed, a strange laugh escaping his lips. "She will bake you many pies! Cakes! Sweet breads!" Maria smiled proudly.

"Just one pie."

The simple request puzzled Eduardo, but he warmly hugged his angel in gratitude. Abel gestured for the door. As the couple walked out, Abel issued an ominous warning.

"Remember, Mr. Ramirez," Abel said. "Tell no one what happened here, not even your children. What I took from your wife... I do not want to give back."

Despite wanting to offer more for his miracle, Eduardo respectfully, somewhat fearfully, agreed to the one pie. The couple walked out into the sun. Carlos followed, but paused at the open door.

"Sorry, Boss," Carlos said in English. "About the money."

"I'd think after nine years you'd know better."

"We coulda used that fifty. That's what I know. We gotta eat, Boss."

Standing in his barren, decrepit room, Abel couldn't argue. "You'll get the first big piece of that pie, my friend."

Carlos nodded and left with the old couple, shutting the door behind him.

* * *

The door to Room 9 opened again. As before, Carlos remained at the doorway as new visitors entered.

Annalisa Vega, a middle-aged Filipino woman, walked in with her son, Roberto, an angry young man just two months shy of his seventeenth birthday. She wore a sundress, while her son proudly wore gang colors in baggy jeans and a tight dress shirt unbuttoned to display his work-in-progress abs.

"You want me to speak to this fool?" Roberto asked his mother in Tagalog, a common Filipino dialect.

"Be nice!" Annalisa barked at him in Tagalog. "This is a man of God!"

Roberto scoffed at the notion. Abel snuffed his cigarette and approached the teen, speaking to him in English. As before, he offered his hand as he introduced himself.

"My name is Abel Grant."

Roberto looked at Abel's extended hand for a moment before taking it. He didn't yet trust the mysterious "angel", nor did he understand what the hell he was doing there.

"Roberto, Annalisa," the young man said, introducing himself and his mother. He grinned as he turned to the large man at the door. "And you're Carlos, right? Respect." Carlos nodded in recognition. Roberto turned his attention back to Abel. "My moms don't speak no English, but she gets it a little bit."

"And I get Filipino a little bit," Abel said, "so we're halfway to an understanding. Now... tell me."

Roberto found it hard to explain, as if it was all nonsense. "My moms says she's been having seizures. She says you can help, that you're some kind of shaman, something like that?"

"Something like that."

"So, do whatever you do, I guess. She wants the seizures gone. It's news to me, but she says they're pretty bad."

Abel studied his guests. He saw the worry on Annalisa's face, how she kept looking at her son, and realized the truth.

"She's not here for any seizures," Abel said.

Roberto stared at his mother, incredulous, until she finally broke her silence. She spoke in Tagalog hurriedly, as if the timing was critical. "His brother! Only eighteen when he joined the gang! Their father's gang!"

"What the fuck is this?" Roberto said, stammering.

"Quiet!" Abel said.

"The police shot him! And he almost died!" Annalisa continued. "Instead, he's in prison. Now my baby boy is on the same path..."

"You lied to me!" her son said, his voice bellowing in a lit fury.

Annalisa spoke fast, Abel somehow understanding it all. "Please, Angel! I know you can't help everyone, but he hasn't yet lost his way. He is still young. Give him the strength to resist the Devil! Bring God to his heart!"

"I don't 'bring' anything," Abel replied in crude Tagalog. "I take away."

"Then take away his anger! It blinds him! It clouds his mind!"

"Fuck all of this!" Roberto yelled. He turned to leave, but Abel quickly grabbed his hand. The teenager cursed, tried to break free. "Get the fuck off me!"

Carlos rushed in and muscled Roberto in a bear hug, easily restraining him. Abel changed his hand-hold until the feeling returned.

Roberto stopped struggling, pointless with Carlos holding him. Once again, Abel felt a heavy weight pressed on him. He lowered to his knees, still clutching the young man's hand.

"I ain't praying wit' you!" Roberto screamed.

"Ain't no one praying!" Abel said as he winced in pain, gripping Roberto's hand tighter. Carlos slowly freed the young man. He offered no resistance.

A moment later, Abel and Roberto released each other. To his shock, Roberto's anger and rage had fallen away. He turned to his mother, a single tear falling down his cheek. He trembled, not sure what just happened. "I don't... I mean... Nanay...?"

Annalisa embraced her son, now flooded with new thoughts, a new perspective, sympathy for his mother's ordeal.

"I'm sorry, Nanay. I'm so sorry!"

Mother and son cried together for the first time in years. Carlos returned to the doorway, clearly touched by the exchange, but trying desperately to hide it. Abel's stone face betrayed a slight smile.

Annalisa looked at Abel. She could barely get her words out. "Thank you, my angel."

"Remember," Abel said, "tell no one what happened here, or the darkness I took away will return."

Annalisa nodded as she reached into her purse. "I know you do not accept money, only what is made by my hands. I hope you will take this." She offered Abel a red rose wrapped around a crucifix. He hesitated, but accepted the kind gesture. "The rose is from my yard. The cross will help you with your work."

"Sure it will," Abel said.

Annalisa and Roberto walked out of the motel room holding hands just as they did years prior when he was still an innocent boy. Carlos followed but once again paused at the door, turning to his boss with a look of curiosity.

"Maybe one day you'll tell me what exactly happens when you hold a man's hand," Carlos said.

"One day."

"Yeah, and one day we won't be squatting in a dead motel. One day we'll buy a full tank, won't have to suck gas outta parked cars no more. Maybe one day we'll hit the road and never come back."

"That's right. One day."

"At least tell me how the hell you were able to talk to that woman," Carlos said. "Since when do you speak Tagalog?"

"You're not the only one who knows Spanish and Filipino."

"Sure, but I was raised with 'em."

"I know a lot more than that. It's part of 'the gift,' if that's what we're calling it now."

Carlos nodded as he considered his boss's cryptic words. He followed mother and son out of the room, shutting the door as they left.

Finally alone, Abel uncovered a shoebox on the bedside table, already filled with miniature bibles, crosses, rosary beads, and pictures of the Virgin Mary.

He carelessly tossed Annalisa's crucifix into the shoebox.

Carlos sat at his office window, headphones on, magazine in hand. The roaring engine of a Dodge Viper - an exotic muscle car - ripped him out of his heavy metal trance as it parked in front of him, next to his lowrider. The driver stepped out, removed his sunglasses, and checked the address on a crumbled note from his coat pocket.

Mr. Brennan, a fifty-year-old Caucasian in a disheveled suit, slammed the door of his Viper. His companion, Mr. Felix, a young Mexican man with a sour face, shirt and tie, joined him as he stumbled up to the office and banged on the window, grabbing Carlos' attention. Brennan looked around the old motel for a moment before speaking in his grizzled, chain-smoker voice. "Damn, boy, is this place even open for business? Looks condemned!"

"You two need a room?" Carlos asked with a grin.

"I need a helluva lot more than that, tough guy." Brennan lifted his dress shirt, exposing his stomach. The sight shocked Carlos.

"Come with me," Carlos said.

In Room 9, Abel picked up his pack of White Knights as if considering another smoke, even though he felt he had no choice. He lit a new cigarette while gazing at a photo in his hand.

In the photo, a tuxedo-clad Abel danced with a beautiful African-American woman glammed up in a flowing white gown. They twirled at a lavish party on a pier. The photo seemed to come alive as he could clearly hear the smooth jazz of that evening, the steady beat of the waves, the chatter of the many party-goers, and the wind across the water. He could smell the perfume on the nape of her neck, the bready champagne on her breath, and the lingering gunpowder from spent fireworks.

A knock on the door halted the beloved memory, ripping him from that pier a lifetime ago.

Carlos entered with Mr. Brennan, who quickly spotted the cigarette.

"At last we meet," Brennan said. "Bum a smoke?"

Abel gave Brennan his newly lit cigarette. He promptly took a long drag.

"Unfiltered White Knights?" Brennan asked. "You really do like to cheat death, my friend." He took his time with another drag. "I'm quitting. Again. Sadly, it just means I don't buy 'em no more."

"My name is Abel Grant." He offered a handshake, but Brennan didn't take it. Instead, he puffed his cigarette with a slightly drunken smile. His voice thundered, as if he owned the joint.

"So, this is the place?" Brennan said. "And you're the guy, right? I mean, THE guy?"

Abel kept his hand out. Brennan laughed at what he saw as a foolish bit of ceremony. He turned to his companion. "Keep an eye on the car, Mr. Felix. They'll strip it skin-and-bones in this shit hole."

Felix nodded and stepped outside. Carlos followed, shutting the door as he left.

Brennan let Abel keep his hand out for a moment before finally taking it. "You call me Brennan."

"Who told you about me, Mr. Brennan?"

"How does this work?" Brennan said, ignoring his host's question. "You shout some voodoo shit? Dance around? Sacrifice a chicken?"

Abel approached his guest, smelling something strong. "Whiskey?"

"Bourbon. Just a touch."

"Perhaps a touch too much," Abel said. "Maybe you should come back tomorrow."

"Ah, but maybe there is no tomorrow. Not for me."

Brennan's tipsy smile faded. Abel stared at the drunk man. He relented and gestured for him to sit on the bed.

"Tell me," Abel said.

"How about I show you?"

Brennan lifted his shirt, revealing his grotesque torso, every inch peppered with large tumors. Abel was aghast, the sight morbid and shocking, though he kept his stone face.

"How long?" Abel asked.

"Years and years, in and out of hospitals, filling doctors' pockets while they spun their wheels. Years and years until I resort to fuckin' voodoo, rumors of a Black miracle worker in a broke down motel."

"You realize I may be unable to help you?"

Brennan tossed a thick roll of cash onto the bed. Abel didn't touch it, didn't even acknowledge it.

"Yeah, yeah," Mr. Brennan said. "I heard you do this shit pro bono. But in my experience, cold hard cash motivates everyone to work harder. Even Black angels."

Carlos entered again, witnessing the rare sight of his boss taken unaware. Abel stood near Brennan and took his hand. As before, he changed his grip several times, waiting for the feeling to come. Brennan sat silently, and for a moment he was a believer, hopeful for a miracle. He was surprised, broken-hearted, when Abel released him and stepped away.

"Mr. Brennan," Abel said. "I'm sorry, but you're beyond my help."

"Try again."

Abel nodded to Carlos to open the door.

"Try. AGAIN."

Failing to intimidate Abel, Brennan's confidence and attitude disappeared as he reduced to a stuttering, desperate man. "This is... bullshit! The stories I heard... you helped far worse!"

"It doesn't matter how bad it is," Abel said. "What matters is how long you've lived with it."

"You wanted to know how I found out about you? Perez. Fuckin' Rodrigo Perez."

Brennan gave Abel a moment to remember Rodrigo. Abel nodded that he did. He remembered every one of the hundreds of souls he helped over his nine years as a divine servant.

Brennan recalled Rodrigo's story with emotion.

"I own warehouses next to St. Nelia. Perez loaded trucks. Brought a box of sweet bread every morning. Nice guy. That was before a forklift clipped him. Goddamn, there was so much blood. His legs were... Doctor said he'd limp for the rest of his life. And man, what a limp." Brennan pulled himself together, buttoning his shirt. "I could've let him go, but I felt for him. You see, I take care of my men. Then one day he comes in brand new, smiling, dancing a jig. Word was he had Jesse Owens's fuckin' legs now. So I asked him about it. He said he just prayed and healed. Not a peep about you."

Brennan gestured for another cigarette. Abel complied, lighting a new one for him. Brennan took another slow drag.

"I got churchy on Rodrigo," Brennan continued, "said that God told me to talk to him, all that bullshit. He finally said 'The Angel' healed him, but he wasn't allowed to tell me who."

"He didn't tell you, did he?"

"Nope. Even after I threatened to deport his ass. So I poked around. Goddamn son, you have touched a lot of fuckin' people around here. And they all say the same thing, that an Angel of God held their hand."

"They're wrong," Abel said. "God left long ago."

Brennan's emotions spiraled as he pulled a gun from his coat. Abel and Carlos froze. Brennan raised the weapon along with his trembling voice.

"Why them?" Brennan asked. "Old women with a foot in the grave? Junkie whores? Homeless bastards with nothing on the horizon?"

Abel remained calm. Carlos stood ready at the door.

"There were many others beyond my help," Abel said, looking at the desperate man with a look of apology.

Mr. Brennan's whimpering took a sharp turn. He suddenly screamed through tears. "You're a sadist! You prey on the superstition of these ignorant fools! Make them believe in you! But your little show, you don't do it for money, you do it for kicks! What kind of twisted fuck are you?"

Brennan quickly walked up to Abel, his gun pointed to his face. Abel looked past the gun and spoke calmly to its owner. "I'm not afraid of that gun, Mr. Brennan, so you can put it away. And maybe you're right and this is all a con. The people I save? Maybe they saved themselves. Maybe they had the strength all along. I'd like to think that. Maybe all they needed was to believe in a miracle." Abel nodded to Carlos to open the door. "And maybe you can find some salvation in that when you leave."

"When I leave," Mr. Brennan laughed. "Might as well leave now." He quickly turned the gun on himself, holding it to his temple.

Carlos rushed him, slapped down the gun as it went off...

BLAM!

Brennan screamed in pain. In the struggle, he shot himself in his side. He clutched his wound as blood poured out.

Upon hearing the gunshot, Mr. Felix ran in. Carlos stopped him as Abel quickly pressed on Brennan's wound with both hands. Instantly, Abel felt the searing pain of the critical wound surge into him.

Carlos picked up Brennan's gun and tucked it in his back pocket. Abel held Brennan tight and close as the injured man continued to struggle and reel from shock. They collapsed to the floor, Abel never letting go. Carlos knelt and wrapped his massive arms around the flailing man, trying to keep him still.

After a tense struggle, Abel finally got the feeling.

Carlos got the feeling as well. After serving his boss for nine years, nearly a decade of faith and trust that the angel's gift was real and not merely a clever mentalist's trick, Carlos got his long-time wish. Entangled with Abel and Brennan on the floor, he became part of the moment.

For the first time, Carlos had the full experience.

The room fell silent, as did the bustling barrio that surrounded the motel. Time slowed to a crawl, with a cowering Brennan and a disoriented Felix nearly frozen in place. The blood from Brennan's ribs ran pitch black, dripping like tar, pushing its way down his legs, landing onto the carpet with a loud, echoing boom.

Carlos felt as if he were kneeling in dense snow, his arms and legs impossibly cold and heavy, his knees bolted to the floor. He saw the colors of the room drain away as everything became a blur, the sounds of his breath and heartbeat pounding and repeating like a bass drum in a grand hall.

Only Abel was in vivid color, his face in focus, as he moved freely within the storm. It crowned his head with an aura of bright light shining from behind, expanding, casting him in silhouette as the ominous glow overtook the room. Though Carlos feared being blinded by the sight, he dared not close his eyes as he took in the spectacle.

Abel released Brennan. Instantly, the room and the rest of the world reverted to their normal state.

Carlos rose to his feet, the jarring transition nearly knocking him over.

Abel placed his head on the corner of the nearby bed. Exhausted, barely able to breathe, he draped his arms onto the mattress.

Brennan remained on his knees, enduring a strange sensation. Mr. Felix rushed to tend to his employer, only to be waved away. Brennan pulled up his shirt to discover an alarming amount of blood without a wound, all traces of the gunshot vanished, though the many tumors remained.

Abel crawled to the bathroom and bowed over the toilet. He spewed a rush of bloody vomit, filling the bowl completely red. He slowly climbed up the sink to stand. A bullet fell from his hand and plunked onto the tile floor. The faucet long dead, Abel washed himself with a gallon jug of water, splashing it onto his face and shoulders.

Mr. Brennan sat stunned speechless as he watched Abel. He realized that what just transpired in that old motel room was indeed a miracle. He knew that the man reeling at the sink, trying to regain himself, truly served a higher power, an audacious claim he'd been told for months. All those poor souls who regaled him with stories of the angel at the Royal Queen Motel had spoke the truth, a truth that a man like Brennan would have never believed if he hadn't been touched by it.

Abel looked up from the sink and saw the realization and hope in Brennan's eyes, saw him slide his fingertips over his cancerous torso in wonder.

"Mr. Brennan," Abel said. "You're still going to die. Just not today, not from that bullet."

Disappointed and dejected, Brennan had no words, but his desperation had left him. He rose to his feet, straightened his blood-soaked shirt and coat, and wandered to the door.

Abel called to him. "Payment, Mr. Brennan."

Confused, Brennan turned to Abel, looked at the two guards staring speechless at him. He spied the roll of cash still sitting unwanted on the bed. He considered it for a moment before pocketing it, instead offering Abel his wristwatch. "The only real Rolex in this part of town. We good?"

"Something you made."

Mr. Brennan thought for a moment. He pulled his wallet from his coat and removed a business card from it. He offered both the watch and the card. "The only thing I ever made is my business. I built it from nothing, brick-by-brick."

Abel reluctantly accepted the payment. He looked at the card: "Brennan Storage and Transport."

"Call me if you need anything," Brennan said. "Anything. Everyone in this neighborhood needs me, eventually. It's the one thing we have in common." He looked to Carlos, who still held his gun in his back pocket. Mr. Felix held his own gun at his side, waiting for his boss's next word.

"You can keep that, too," Brennan said, eyeing his old gun. He nodded to his companion. Mr. Felix opened the door, and the two men stepped outside.

Rather than follow them, Carlos promptly shut the door, remaining with his boss. He peered through the window blinds to watch them drive away.

Abel collapsed onto the bed and stared at the cracked ceiling. "You still want to know what happens when I hold a man's hand?"

Carlos had no ready response. He opened the door and gazed out at the decaying barrio, at the empty parking lot baking in the sun that would soon have more grief-stricken visitors who heard about the angel at the old, abandoned motel on the edge of the St. Nelia District.

"One day, Boss."

Carlos left Abel alone in the room

Abel looked at Brennan's Rolex, nearly forgetting it was in his hand. He admired the gaudy trinket for a moment before tossing it carelessly into the shoebox.

# 2

# Broken Door

The setting sun and rising moon briefly shared the overcast sky as Abel left the Royal Queen Motel, his shoebox in hand. He walked past five blocks of shuttered motels and boarded storefronts, heading north along Arrowhead Boulevard, turning west through the rows of warehouses and tenements of H Street. The St. Nelia District had often been called the barely beating heart of La Figueira's Old Downtown, but Abel saw it as teeming with life and wouldn't live anywhere else, even if he had the twenty-eight dollars in his wallet a thousandfold. Such desperate inner-city streets were where he was meant to be, not the well-to-do boulevards far north or the opulent gated communities along the bluffs, the kinds of privileged areas he used to call home before he begrudgingly discovered his gift.

To one side of the narrow street ran several sets of interstate railroad tracks serving miles-long freight trains that would rumble by throughout the evening and into the night. On the other side stood a row of narrow, low-rise apartment buildings whose architectural beauty had long been obscured by decades of decay. Most were vacant and filled with squatters, while the active few housed families in cramped, poorly lit studios that often lacked indoor plumbing and proper ventilation, a slum lord's wet dream.

The many vagrants, street hustlers, and impoverished families greeted Abel as he continued down the cracked sidewalk, offering discrete warm smiles to the angel who once saved them, forgetting their lives of struggle for a fleeting moment. Abel returned their greetings with a slight nod as he approached his home, the North Star Arms. The old three-story building's lofty name came from the fact that the neighborhood once stood as La Fig's affluent northern suburb before seventy years of urban sprawl turned it into the much maligned south side.

The final friendly face Abel saw during his walks home always belonged to Marci Williams, a middle-aged Mexican-American woman with olive skin and wavy brown hair, who sold gas at the Quick Stop for four hours each morning and sold herself from the front steps of the North Star for six hours each night. Though he frowned upon her nightly vocation, he respected her and accepted her choice, even if he worried for her safety with each sunset. Like the other citizens of H Street, Marci felt her hard life fade whenever she saw her jovial neighbor coming down the sidewalk.

"Miss Marci," Abel said as he reached the stairs.

"Wassap, Abe? Another day, another dollar?" Marci's bright tone and wide eyes were quickly tarnished by the sight of fresh bruises across her face. "Like, you wanna spend that dollar for once?"

Abel gently touched her face with his palm. "No, but I'll give it to you."

Marci considered the gesture, but dismissed it with a playful grin. "Forget it. Like, you ain't got no dollar." She wasn't aware of Abel's divine power. All she knew was that he survived week-to-week as she did. Abandoning her proposition, she scooted aside to reveal bouquets of flowers and Virgin Mary candles sitting together on the top step, gifts from the community for Abel's hard work as a handyman, or so she believed.

"These have been here all day," she said. "Real pretty. I took a rose, if that's cool."

"Take it all."

"Nah. Can't eat flowers and Virgin Marys."

"I got the reverend's famous albondigas soup in the fridge."

Marci winced at the offer. She'd had that soup before. "Ugh. Can't eat that either!"

Abel gathered the candles and entered the building, leaving the flowers for Marci or anyone else to take.

"G'night, Abe. Like, don't party too hard."

Marci turned back to the street, waiting for the inevitable Lexus or Buick from the north side of town to pull up.

Within the North Star Arms, Abel climbed up two flights of stairs to the third floor. He heard the lives of his neighbors as he walked down the long hall to his apartment at the end. Couples fought, rap music thumped, TVs blared, children ran across hardwood floors. He approached his door and found it a few inches ajar. Rather than feel alarmed, he felt frustrated, his recent repair request still not completed. As he muttered a curse, he heard a door open behind him.

Armen Hagopian, a grayed old man in wrinkled overalls, stood in the hall in front of his apartment by the stairs, his door labeled "Resident Manager."

"Armen, when are you going to fix this damn door? Someone could walk in here anytime and steal everything."

"Nothing to steal," Armen said in his thick Persian accent. He wasn't wrong.

Abel could only stare at the old man and laugh in disbelief. "Come on, this should be an easy fix."

"Parts on order. I told you."

"Yeah, two weeks ago! It's a race between your rare door parts and the thief who's going to rob me while I'm away or kill me in my sleep!"

"Buy dog." Armen locked the three deadbolts on his door and headed downstairs.

Abel entered his apartment and shut the door, shoving a chair against the doorknob. From where he stood, he could see everything he owned in one glance around his studio. A ripped sofa sat along a wall beside a small desk. A kitchenette occupied a corner next to the one window facing the street below, comprising a short counter, a single stove burner, a refrigerator, and a Formica dining table with one vinyl chair. The walls were covered in stained, peeling, floral wallpaper, all bare except for a single framed drawing, an impressive winged angel hovering in the clouds, rendered in the style of graffiti art. It hung centered above the sofa as his most prized possession.

The hardwood floor creaked with his every footstep as he walked to his desk and placed the shoebox between a small lamp and an old record player, functional but too damaged to fetch a price at a pawn shop. He reached into the shoebox and fished out Brennan's Rolex, taking a moment to admire the shiny gold trinket in his hand before tossing it back in. He clicked on the lamp and placed his cherished photo at its base, his night of dancing on a pier in another life. Still fixed on the woman in the white gown, he reached for the record player and turned it on.

Bessie Smith's classic "Baby Won't You Please Come Home" filled the room, the legendary jazz singer's thick, rich voice crooning over the pops and cracks of the vintage recording. From the moment the delicate piano arrangement began, an African-American woman appeared behind Abel, sitting on the sofa in a familiar flowing white gown.

Abel turned to the couch to the specter he knew as his late wife, Regina Grant. Playing the jazz classic on his old turntable always summoned her, and though he couldn't actually see his beloved, he could feel her presence and hear her satin gown shift as she crossed her legs at the knee.

"How many did you save today?" Regina asked, always the first to speak. She rose from the sofa and walked about the studio apartment, her footsteps silent on the rickety hardwood floor.

Abel remained at his desk, watching the record spin. "Eight, though I'd argue how many of them are saved."

"You short-sell yourself."

"You can glue together a shattered bottle, but it's never truly saved."

"Now you're short-selling them." She looked out the window at H Street below. "I didn't marry a pessimist."

"He should have chosen you. Not me."

"Not this again," she said with a sigh. "And I haven't heard you say 'He' for a while now."

"He. She. It. They. Whatever."

Regina walked to the fridge and pulled out a bottle of beer. She placed it on the kitchenette table. "Have a drink, baby."

Abel picked up his cherished photo, rose from his desk, and took the lone seat at the table. He popped open the beer with the palm of his hand and took a sip. Regina stood behind him.

"A man came to me today," Abel said to the room, not sure where his late wife stood. "He was bombarded with tumors. I knew right away he was a lost cause."

"But you tried anyway."

"Yes, but he'd been sick a long time, and he wasn't a believer."

"Sure he was," Regina said in her soothing, melodic voice, not unlike Bessie Smith's ongoing tune. "When you held his hand, in that blink of an eye, he was whatever he needed to be."

"He offered money. A lot of money. I could've taken it to Reverend Dean."

Regina scoffed at the notion, a dismissal that stung Abel. "You could have also taken it to the bar."

"He gave me a Rolex instead. I could always take that to the bar. A lot of bars."

"You won't."

"I'm saying I could."

"You couldn't."

Regina knelt beside him and looked into his eyes. He hadn't seen her face during their nightly encounters - not since their tragic night in that forsaken ravine - but he could feel whenever she looked directly at him.

"You can lie to yourself all night, Abel. You can lie to Carlos, to the reverend, to the folks who seek your gift, but you can't lie to me. I know what's in your mind."

"Because that's where you are, Regina. In my mind."

The classic jazz song ended, and the turntable reset. By the time the needle lowered into its docked position, Regina was gone.

The city noise returned, a booming contrast to the calm during the gentle song. Abel sat alone at his dining table and chugged his beer. He stared at the photo in his hand, at Regina dancing with him on the pier. He walked back to his desk, placed the photo at the base of the lamp, and shut off the light.

# 3

# Judge of Character

The line of homeless people and impoverished families stretched around the perimeter of the small parking lot. The early morning sun peeked over the roof, blinding everyone who wasn't standing in the shadow of the large cross cutting through the light.

The Community United Church of the Beloved Saint Nelia - known simply as "St. Nelia's Church" - received two trucks an hour before, a rare double delivery for their biweekly distribution. The first truck came from the La Figueira Food Bank, bringing canned and boxed food, and surplus fruits and vegetables from the farm region north of the city. The second truck came from Metro Community Thrift, offering a cargo of new and used clothes and sundries.

The two box trucks were parked side-by-side, their rear doors open for Reverend Dean McCall and his volunteers to unload. They'd separated the food into "care packages," each box a week's worth of food for a household of four. The donated clothes hung on wheeled wardrobe racks for folks to sift through, all organized by size.

Reverend Dean was a Caucasian man of 45, always in blue jeans and sneakers, his trim black hair parted to the right and salt-and-pepper beard hanging halfway down his clergy collar. His handsome features and genuine smile were a welcome sight to his flock even before the trucks arrived. Along with the donated goods, he offered styrofoam cups of coffee to the adults and hot chocolate to the children.

After a twenty-minute walk from the North Star Arms, Abel walked diagonally across the church's parking lot, past the three-hundred-plus in line, the sunrise reflecting off his eyeglasses. He carried his shoebox under his arm as he looked at all the needy faces, many of whom he'd met privately at the motel, and many more yet to come. As sternly instructed, those who knew him as their angel kept his miraculous gift a secret or risk the return of their ailments.

Abel felt a firm slap on his back and immediately knew whose hand now rested on his shoulder.

"Good morning, Abe," Reverend Dean said in his usual boisterous voice. "Such a good morning."

"If you say so, Reverend." After losing hours of sleep to his cruel nightmares - as he often did - Abel's head felt foggy and thick, his legs heavy like logs, and he envied the reverend's spirited nature at such an early hour.

"What treasures have we today?" Reverend Dean peeked into Abel's shoebox like a kid rummaging for a prize. He paused upon finding the gold Rolex watch and held it up curiously like a misfit toy.

"You like it?" Abel asked.

"A thing like this, it's not a matter of liking it, Abe. It's not even about telling the time. You wear it to make a statement." He returned the decadent watch to the shoebox.

"I figure you could pawn it. Better you do it than me."

"You sure you don't want it? It's an exquisite watch."

"Lead me not into temptation, Reverend. I don't need a gold-plated 'statement' strapped to my wrist, and I certainly don't want to know the time."

"Then how about a cup of coffee? It'll pair well with the five packs of cigarettes you're likely to cough through today."

"You know me too well."

The reverend gestured to his volunteers that he and Abel would be heading inside.

"I don't meant to put you out, Reverend."

"No worries, they have everything covered. Let's step into my office. Got a personal pot of burnt French Roast waiting for us."

The interior of St. Nelia's Church was modest but well maintained, its small entry room lined with stone pillars, statuary, and three doorways. A set of double doors sat opened to the large chapel ahead. The doorway to the right led to the kitchen, bathrooms, and storage rooms, while the doorway to the left led to the offices and classrooms. The church sat empty and silent at this time of day, so quiet that the soft sound of a paintbrush could be heard.

Inside the chapel, Arlo Rosewood knelt beside the rear pews varnishing its oak trim. Even on his knees, he seemed taller than most. The large man looked rugged for his advanced age, an old cowboy with his white hair combed back over a small bald spot. He wore a plaid flannel shirt, jeans, and boots, all spotted with dried paint and wood varnish. His massive, hairy arms slid the brush with care to avoid further spilling varnish on the aisle's carpet runner. Arlo nodded hello to Abel as he entered with the reverend.

"Got you working already, Arlo?" Abel asked.

"Boss is a goddamn slave driver," Arlo said in his deep, tired voice.

"Language, Arlo," Reverend Dean said with a smile.

The two men continued through the left door and entered the reverend's office, a small, cluttered room with a desk, file cabinet, dozens of photos of the congregation pinned to the walls, and an old coffee maker sitting atop a bookshelf. Reverend Dean poured two mugs of coffee as Abel took a seat in front of the desk, setting his shoebox on his lap.

"How was it yesterday?" Reverend Dean asked.

"I saw a few folks."

"That's all? Nothing else to report?" The reverend handed his friend a coffee and took his seat behind the desk.

"These friendly coffee talks are not 'reports,' Reverend."

"Ah, yes, I forgot. You report to no one."

"No offense to your chosen vocation."

"No offense taken, but let's remember, son, it wasn't my chosen anything. *He* chose this life for me, and for that I'm forever grateful, in this life and the next."

"Sure, Reverend. Either way, nothing to 'report' today."

"Not even when a man pulls a gun on you?"

Abel shouldn't have felt surprised by the blunt question. Reverend Dean had many eyes and ears across the district, including those of Abel's most devout and closest confidant.

"So, you heard about that." Abel sipped his burnt coffee. "Goddamn, this coffee is shit."

"Language!"

"Sorry, but your ancient coffee machine is ready for its next life."

"You're worse than Arlo, you know that?"

"Does Carlos tell you everything?"

Reverend Dean had a ready reply, but stopped himself, unsure about outing his source. "Carlos tells me what I need to know. That was *his* report. He said a 'rich guy' threw a tantrum, pulled out a gun. I assume the Rolex was his?"

"He offered me a roll of cash that could choke a horse."

"I assume you turned it down."

"I don't take money, Reverend."

"That's noble, I suppose, but I know you desperately need it. I know you and Carlos barely survive day-to-day. I know the motel is closed and that he steals for you. He has to. You need to eat, son."

"Folks give us food enough. He steals gas, mostly. Light a match, the man will breath fire."

"Despite what people say, money isn't the root of all evil. It's greed. It's what men choose to do with money, what they'll do to get it, and the feeling that it's never enough."

"I get it. Still, I don't take money."

"Well, those people out there will take it. A little goes a long way here."

"No doubt, but I don't take money, not even from those who can afford to throw it away. Especially them." Abel took another sip of his burnt coffee. He walked to the coffee maker and added cream and sugar. "You know Rodrigo Perez?"

"You mean 'Rigo'?" Reverend Dean asked, concerned. "Yes, I know him."

"The 'rich guy' said Rodrigo helped lead him to me. Makes me uneasy."

"Rigo is fine, last I heard."

"I'm sure he is, but I'm getting that Texas feeling all over again. I'm not in the business of helping self-entitled fat cats. Still, I don't think Rodrigo outed me." Abel let the room fall silent, waiting for the reverend's tense response.

"It wasn't me, if that's what you're suggesting."

"What about Cowboy Frankenstein in the chapel?"

"Arlo?" Reverend Dean said with a laugh. "No, I trust him completely."

"Perhaps you trust too easily."

"Arlo is a good man, and I'm a superb judge of character. It's why you're sitting here."

"It's not his character I doubt."

"Perhaps you doubt too easily."

"No argument there." Abel returned to his seat with his newly sweetened coffee. He saw the anticipation on his friend's face, knowing there was more to tell. "This guy, Brennan, waved a fistful of cash around, asking about me, and somebody held out his hand."

Both men were now concerned. They agreed years before, when Abel first arrived in La Figueira and walked into St. Nelia's Church to confide his gift, that they would help the community together, with the reverend carefully vetting candidates to send to the Royal Queen Motel. They swore to help those most in need, and to keep it quiet and under control.

"I'll put the feelers out," Reverend Dean said. "As for this 'Brennan,' I might know him, too."

"You might know him?" Abel asked, confused. "A guy with a Dodge Viper doesn't park it anywhere near St. Nelia."

"The name sounds familiar. That's all."

"Look into it. I don't have to remind you how this can play out. If the Haves find out about me, the Have-Nots are fucked, pardon my heathen tongue."

"I wouldn't lose sleep over it, son. One man is just one man."

"Is that how you preach about Jesus?"

Reverend Dean offered no response as his friend downed the rest of his coffee in one agonizing gulp. "The cream and sugar didn't help?"

"It was shit before. Now it's sweet, creamy shit."

The reverend grimaced at the curse words, giving up on correcting Abel. "We'll work this out. Don't lose faith, Abe."

"Too late, Reverend." Abel set his mug on the desk and rose to his feet. "Look, I don't care who told him about me. You, your gorilla cowboy, one of the sheep from your flock. I just want more discretion when you send folks my way. Just vet them a little more carefully. Understand?"

"Understood."

"I'm also a superb judge of character. I will turn people away."

Reverend Dean smirked at what he knew was a bluff. Abel set the shoebox on the desk and headed for the door.

"Do me a favor, Abe. Grab a box of food on your way out. You and Carlos need to eat something more than the tributes of pies and cakes."

"I'll do that, and you do me a favor. When you pawn that Rolex, buy yourself a new coffee machine."

Abel grabbed an empty shoebox from the book shelf and walked out of the office. Reverend Dean picked up the Rolex and put it on, admiring it on his wrist for a moment before placing it in his desk drawer.

# 4

# Five-Hundred Horses

During the winter of 2011, nearly ten years before arriving in La Figueira and the abandoned Royal Queen Motel, Abel Grant lived 1,400 miles away in Austin, Texas, with his wife, Regina Grant. Their home was a spacious mid-century design of brick and glass, inspired by Frank Lloyd Wright and fit for a magazine spread. Its tall ceilings, sharp angles, and non-parallel walls offered perfect acoustics for a pair of jazz artists. A baby grand piano sat on the polished concrete floor. Concert posters hung on the walls, both classic and contemporary, each autographed by jazz greats like Chick Corea, Herbie Hancock, Camila Meza, Miles Davis, Esperanza Spalding, and Bessie Smith.

Abel entered the grand foyer wearing a tuxedo, platinum cufflinks, and a gold Rolex watch to match his gold cross necklace. He sat at his piano and sipped cognac from a highball glass, swirling its single ice cube, careful to savor the French spirit and set it on a cork coaster. Sliding his hand across the top of the baby grand, he lifted the cover from the keys, folded it forward and down, and allowed his fingertips to explore. Abel expertly played Leadbelly's "Where Did You Sleep Last Night?" singing the intro of the somber blues standard in a decent baritone before letting the piano take over.

*"My girl, my girl, don't lie to me*
*Tell me where did you sleep last night*
*In the pines, in the pines*
*Where the sun don't ever shine*
*I would shiver the whole night through"*

Regina smiled at the familiar song as she descended the stairs toward him. Without missing a note, Abel turned to her and admired the long, flowing white gown she chose for their evening out.

"Gloves or no gloves?" Regina asked, holding up a pair of long, white satin gloves. He hadn't heard her, still fixated on how the tight upper portion of her outfit accentuated her figure.

"Look... at... you," Abel said. "Are you real or are you a vision?" He stared at her as his fingers kept playing the delicate tune.

"Be quiet, Abe." Regina never could take a compliment, not even from her husband of twelve years. "It's just an old gown I dug out of the closet."

"Sure, and 'Round Midnight' is just an old song." He seamlessly transitioned to playing the Thelonious Monk classic.

"You're comparing an outfit I threw together to T-Monk? Mighty high praise coming from you."

"Just saying, there are only so many women in the world who can wear a dress like that."

Regina reached the foyer and stood before a framed wall mirror to put on her earrings. "And there's only so many men who can take it off at the end of the night."

"Only one man, you mean." Abel grinned slyly. "Lady, you keep talking like that and we'll never make it to the party..."

"Dammit!" Regina whipped her right hand back, dropping one of her earrings to the floor.

Abel rushed from his piano to tend to her. He picked up the small gold spade earring and saw blood on his fingertips. "What the hell? Are you hurt?"

"I cut myself on that thing." Regina sucked on her right index finger. "Please tell me I didn't ruin my dress."

Abel scanned his wife. Miraculously, not a drop of blood landed on the bright white gown. He gave her the earring and took a quick look at the cut. "Let me fix that for you." He walked to the bathroom under the stairs and returned with a cotton swab and a bandage. "Let Nurse Abel patch you up."

"Thank you, Nurse Abel."

Abel swabbed alcohol on her finger's deep cut and wrapped it with the small latex bandage. "Good to go."

"How perfect," Regina said with a groan. "Looks like I'm wearing gloves after all." She turned back to the mirror and carefully put the earring on, followed by the pair of long satin gloves, pulling them up to her elbows.

Abel placed his hands around her waist and kissed her exposed shoulders, running his palms down her arms. "You know, I think you should lie down after an injury like that."

"Stop it, Abel."

"Do we really have to go to this shindig?"

"We kinda have to, since I'm singing."

"For Phillip."

"For everybody. There's gonna be at least a hundred folks expecting entertainment, many of whom work in the industry. Could be good for us."

"I suppose we are committed." Abel nodded and released his wife with one more kiss. He walked to a wet bar behind his piano. "How come you never sing at my birthday parties?"

"Oh, I don't know, maybe 'cause you never have birthday parties? We go out for dinner, we come home for wine, and we listen to old blues records in bed."

"Sounds like a perfect evening to me, and it's what your birthday boy wants, right?"

"Well, tonight Phillip is the birthday boy, so be good."

"I always am, madam." He slid his highball glass and coaster across the piano to the bar and poured a drink. "Remy Martin to start?"

Regina laughed as she touched up her make-up in the mirror. "Put that down! There'll be plenty at the party."

"But there won't be Remy Martin. I know because Phillip Crescenzo, Esquire, doesn't drink cognac. He's a dedicated bourbon man. It's no wonder he and I don't connect."

"And how do you know what Phillip Crescenzo will and won't have? You go out drinking with my agent without me?"

Abel slugged his glass of cognac and promptly poured another. "I know because he has a bottle of Louis XIII Legacy unopened on his shelf. Fifteen-grand a bottle and he's never touched it, never brought it to the club." Abel downed his drink almost as quickly as the last. "A rare Remy like that and he ain't never gonna taste it. Shame."

"Guess you ain't never gonna taste it neither," Regina said, teasing. "Truly a shame."

Abel poured another drink, clumsily spilling a little on his baby grand, promptly wiping it up with a handkerchief from his breast pocket. "That's why I'm having my little sippy sip now. Seeing that damn crystal decanter on his shelf kills me."

Regina picked up her clutch purse from a hook under the mirror and walked to the door. "I'd hardly call shooting down three glasses in a row 'a little sippy sip.' Keys, please." She held out her palm.

Abel slowly slurped his drink as if to disprove his wife's observation. His tipsy laugh betrayed his attempt to hide his fuzzy head. "Keys? Since when can you handle 500 horses? Or drive stick?"

"Since never, but right now I'm the most capable driver in the room, and I know you had another one earlier. So give me the keys, wino."

"Shows what you know. I had a duet before this trio."

Abel finished his drink and set the glass on the wet bar. He made the Sign of The Cross on his forehead and chest, kissed the crucifix on his necklace, and handed his wife the car keys. His theatrics made her laugh.

"We're gonna be listening to Bessie in the car," Regina said. "I need to get the lyrics down if I'm gonna sing it right."

"Oh Lord, I'm sick of that song."

"Don't you blaspheme Bessie!"

"You know that song, baby! You're gonna knock it out of the park!"

"Driver picks the music, remember?"

Abel recalled the strict rule he made long ago when they first met. They took turns driving during their first dates and made a little game out of who got to control the car stereo. It was then that they fell in love while discovering their mutual love of jazz and blues.

"Driver picks the music," Abel said, relenting. "I know."

"Don't blame me, blame Remy Martin."

Abel and Regina walked out the door to a shiny red Corvette parked in their semi-circular driveway, the sleek sports coupe on cobblestone wet and slick from a light drizzle. Regina fumbled to start the engine and shift into gear but quickly got it running and down the driveway.

After they turned a corner at the end of the street and disappeared from view of the house, the quiet of the suburb split apart by sounds that pierced the air though they came from hundreds of miles away...

A distant car horn blared...

A flock of birds scattered...

The horn bowed to a deep dirge...

The wind howled down a ravine...

The chaos rose to to an unnerving, deafening pitch...

* * *

Abel woke up in his studio apartment at dawn, to the harsh sound of the sustaining horn of a car alarm on the street below. He sat up in his sofa bed and took a moment to reorient himself, his haunting dream of the last night he saw Regina alive fading fast, though not fast enough. Through the head and body aches of a mild hangover, he caught sight of empty beer bottles on his kitchenette counter and cursed himself for losing his love, almost wishing he'd never met her to begin with. Perhaps then she'd still be singing blues standards at clubs and events, her voice floating across the stage, over the audience, and into the night.

He passed the door on route to the bathroom and noticed the wooden chair he propped against the knob had been moved slightly, the door no longer flush with its frame. Someone tried to open the door while he was asleep. He knew it was likely a squatter looking for a new spot. They often searched the old tenements of H Street in search of a vacant apartment. There were plenty of them, yet another reason Armen needed to fix that broken door.

Abel once spent the night at the motel after exhausting himself receiving twelve visitors - the most he'd ever healed in a single day - and came home the following morning to find his ceiling fan gone, his refrigerator empty, and a homeless man in his shower. Without assigning blame for the thefts, Abel allowed the man his shower and even gave him a disposable razor and a fresh change of clothes before politely telling him to leave and seek aid at St. Nelia's Church.

Reverend Dean maintained a limited shelter with hot showers and clean toilets behind the chapel, though he always hesitated spreading word of it. He wanted to personally choose the unfortunate souls who took refuge at the church, just as he vetted those who sought the angel rumored to be in the area.

Abel shut the door and shoved the chair firmly against the doorknob again. He looked up at the exposed wires dangling from a hole in the ceiling where his fan used to be and knew that desperate people would keep sifting through his meager belonging when given the chance, taking anything that wasn't bolted down. It was a small miracle that his turntable and collection of rare, vintage jazz and blues records still sat on the desk, though he had to replace the lamp five times.

He took a long shower, shaved, brushed his teeth, and ate a breakfast of toasted white bread with strawberry jam. He savored the moments of his morning routine as little luxuries that kept him grounded and grateful to be alive after the debacle that forced him to flee Texas, never to see his beloved Austin again. Abel bowed his head and said grace over his simple plate of toast and jam, giving thanks to Carlos, Reverend Dean, and the citizens of the St. Nelia District for respecting his privacy and protecting his identity, and though he spoke to God in his prayer, he refused to thank Him as well, still hurt and angry from the cruel twist of fate in the woods nearly ten years before.

As he prepared to leave for the day, more worried than ever about that busted doorknob, he remembered a trick Carlos once taught him. He took a matchbook from his desk and stepped out into the hallway. He wedged two matches between the door and the door frame, their red sulfur heads pressed together, and gently shut the door. The matches would hold the door in place, making it appear securely shut at a glance. If someone entered his apartment while he was away, the two matches would strike each other and fall spent to the hall floor, offering him a crude warning of robbery or an intruder.

Abel wasn't sure why he felt the need to employ such amateur spycraft as there wasn't much to protect, as Armen had pointed out, but he couldn't shake the feeling that a little more security was suddenly warranted.

Carlos had been at the Royal Queen Motel since 7:00 a.m. He always arrived an hour ahead of his boss to ensure that the abandoned property was completely vacant. Most days, he shooed away vagrants in the parking lot or squatters that spent the night in one of the rooms. He sometimes encountered groups of hardened men who'd never heard of the angel nor would ever care, but few dared to defy Carlos Cruz. The poor fools who challenged the towering former gangster soon regretted it as Carlos took his vow seriously, ready to instantly strike down anyone who posed a threat to their ongoing mission and to the well being of his boss. By the time Abel walked onto the lot at eight o'clock, the interlopers were always well on their way elsewhere.

Carlos Joaquin Cruz was a top lieutenant of the Lincoln Heights Guerreros, a large gang well known on the south side of La Fig. In his youth, he drove his lowrider Impala down Arrowhead Avenue with his associates, childhood friends Ozzy Castillo and Ignacio Valle, often joined by his teenage nephew, Lino. Carlos served as the gang's Lead Enforcer, extorting monthly protection money from the few local businesses that stuck it out through the neighborhood's decline. He rarely had to resort to violence, for most of the business owners were undocumented Mexican immigrants, or had friends or family who were, none of whom felt they had any voice in America, any recourse in the grip of organized crime. The others who had their papers still offered no resistance, for few dared to defy Carlos Cruz.

Seeing young Lino Cruz following in his footsteps instilled no sense of pride. Instead, seeing his nephew rise in the ranks of the Guerreros gave him pause. It was one thing to lean on the owner of a struggling restaurant, but another thing entirely to watch his fifteen-year-old apprentice copy his intimidation tactics. The boy had traded his sterling report card and wide-open future for a position in the gang, and Carlos knew he did it not for any street cred or gangster glory but to simply put a smile on his uncle's face. Carlos did smile with pride, if only when Ozzy and Ignacio were present. Secretly, he pondered a way out for Lino and himself. Sadly, it wouldn't be until they attended their cousin's wedding 1,400 miles away that Carlos would get his wish, and he and Lino would see the brutal end of their criminal lives.

When Abel arrived at the motel at eight sharp, he saw Carlos washing his lowrider, its doors wide open to let the booming stereo fill the property with bass-heavy rap. Abel found his friend's careful attention to the car's appearance curious as it had suffered scratches, dings, and spots of rust from years out in the elements, all masking an engine with three leaks and a high-pitched metallic whine that sounded like a running circular saw dropped to the pavement. It seemed a lost cause to meticulously maintain a car in such poor condition, but it served as sentiment and ceremony more than common sense.

Carlos noticed Abel standing behind him. "Got nine coming today. Maybe more."

"Christ, it's like the reverend put us in the Yellow Pages."

Carlos reached into the front seat of the car and pulled out a fast food bag. He handed Abel a cheeseburger.

"The most important meal of the day," Abel said, hesitant to unwrap his greasy breakfast.

"Don't blame the reverend. Word always spreads, no matter what. We knew it was coming. First things first, you gotta eat."

"You talk with him a lot, don't you?"

As Abel took a bite of his burger, Carlos could see the fatigue on his boss's face. "You good? We can shut down today if you're not feeling up to it."

"No," Abel said. "Let them come."

Abel slammed a pack of White Knights in his palm, readied his first cigarette, and took his cheeseburger to Room 9, where he'd be holed up for the day.

Ten hours later, the sun set behind the motel as Carlos stepped out of the room with two young Latinas. They smiled, wiping away tears, one of them pushing an empty wheelchair - no longer needed.

"Are you sure you want nothing else?" one of the women asked Carlos. She held a roll of cash, nervous about taking it out of her purse again. "We saved our money for three months for this day. It seems wrong to come back tomorrow with just a plate of chicken empanadas."

"Make it a big ass plate."

"I promise, it'll be enough to feed him for a week."

"That'll do." Carlos winced at the thought of food instead of cash yet again, but felt grateful that they were at least coming back with protein rather than the usual flowers or pastries. It often proved difficult to make a meal out of pie and cookies.

He watched the young woman tuck the roll of cash back into her purse, thinking back to a time when he'd have snatched that money before a word was said, but he remembered his promise to Abel, even as it pained him to commit to it. He recalled his boss's steadfast command, repeated almost daily.

*We take disease. We take pain and suffering.*

*We don't take money.*

After a final hug from both of them, the two women got in their car and drove away. Carlos returned to his office window and spotted something odd across the street.

Two men in suits sat on a bus stop bench across Arrowhead Avenue, watching the motel. In their intent scrutiny, their eyes met his, and a stare-down ensued. Before

Carlos could make his way toward them, Abel emerged from Room 9 for his evening trek home. He looked exhausted, his every step a focused effort, as he carried another shoebox filled with tribute. He waved at his friend as he headed down the sidewalk. Carlos ran after him.

"Hey, boss, we ain't done yet."

"Yes, we are. We push it any more, Big Man, you'll be mopping me up off the floor."

"But we got two more."

"Tell them to come back tomorrow morning. I'll meet with them first."

"Alright, but what about those guys?" Carlos looked back at the bus stop across the street, but the two men were gone. "Boss, there was two suits over there mad-doggin' me."

"Looks like you scared them off. Good night, Carlos."

Abel walked home, leaving Carlos to wonder where the men disappeared to.

# 5

# The Farm

The streets were shiny from a light evening rain when Abel came home to the North Star Arms. As always, he saw Marci standing on the front steps of the building. Sometimes he saw her talking with a potential client. That night, he saw two men with her on the top step. They wore dark gray suits and black shoes, and traded small talk about the neighborhood, favorite music, and whether she knew anything about fine wine.

As Abel reached the building, the two men ended their conversation, nodded goodbye, and walked across the street. Marci turned to him with a warm smile but didn't receive one in return. Instead of his usual bad joke, inspirational quote, or nugget of useless trivia - she often called him a "human fortune cookie" - Abel wore a stone expression and moved at a glacial pace. Marci saw him slump home like that many times before, and knew he felt absolutely spent from another of his long days repairing faucets, painting walls, unclogging toilets, and anything else asked of him. Seeing him so often exhausted from nine-to-five blue-collar labor squashed her absurd suspicion that he was the holy man rumored to be working miracles in the district, working undercover, erasing disease and reversing impending death. The sight of him dragging his feet up the stone steps made her laugh for ever entertaining the wild notion.

Marci trotted down the stairs in her heels and offered an arm to her friend. Abel refused at first, but changed his mind two agonizing steps up, glad for the assistance.

"You don't look so good, Abe."

"Sadly, I could say the same."

He eyed yet another new bruise on her face, darker and wider than the last. She turned away with a dismissive grunt.

"Goes with the profession," she said in an irate tone, sick of people looking out for her.

"So get a new profession."

Their exchange felt routine, but if Abel's response sounded like a suggestion before, it resonated like insistence now. With each bruise he saw, each black eye and busted lip and torn blouse, he imagined her being abused by one of her more sadistic clients who paid extra for "the rough stuff." Abel could never reveal that he felt her every wound, experiencing her assaults secondhand, or that each harrowing moment brought him closer to taking action. He knew that butting into her life would throw away the trust between them - while also blowing his cover - painting her as a damsel in distress unable to endure her chosen life. She understood his concern but resented his fatherly instinct to protect her. Marci never needed a white knight before and winced at the thought.

Ready to collapse, Abel wouldn't intervene that night, but knew it was inevitable, just around the corner.

Resting on the top step for a moment, he watched the two men in suits get in a sedan across the street. They didn't drive away or even start the engine. There merely sat in their car and listened to the stereo.

"Wanna go in for a drink?" Marci asked, letting her brief frustration go.

"Marci..."

"I ain't workin' you, alright? Just coffee and company. Like, I think we both need it right now."

* * *

Abel sat on the couch in the middle of Marci's apartment. Its layout was identical to his studio next door, with its weathered hardwood floors and single window offering a view of the street. Otherwise, it looked vastly different because of the dense decor. Potted plants sat in every corner. Posters of garden landscapes covered every wall. Sheer lace curtains dangling from the ceiling visually separated the kitchenette and dining table from the living room space.

Marci stood in the kitchenette, waiting on a microwave oven. She had changed out of her working girl skirt and into jogging pants topped with a thick, oversized sweater.

Underneath it all, she wore a full set of thermals and two pairs of thick wool socks. Though she was willing to endure the cold night in search of her next client, she couldn't bear to shiver within the walls of her home.

After the microwave beeped, Abel watched her remove a large Pyrex mug of water from it and prepare coffee for two, with sugar, cream, and heavy pours of whiskey.

"Two Irish coffees coming right up," she said, mimicking a busy bartender.

"Easy on the Irish, please."

"Hope you're okay with decaf." The condensation from her breath hung in the chilly air as she spoke. "And I had to use the microwave. Like, the gas has been out for three weeks." She brought the two coffees to the couch, handed one to Abel, and sat beside him. She cupped her mug in her hands, rubbing it for warmth. "And it's just instant."

Abel took a sip and smiled. "It's instantly good."

Marci laughed at the dumb joke but paused upon hearing a creak in the floorboards. She turned toward it for a moment, concerned, but let it go.

"Marci, if you ever need a hot shower, I'm gone most of the day."

"Cold water is the least of my problems. Tell me about Dean."

"The reverend? What do you want to know?"

"What's he like? He's good lookin' for an older guy, sorta, but he's way too into Jesus."

Abel laughed at the odd observation. "It goes with his profession."

"I get it, but you guys friends or what?"

"I suppose."

"For reals? I only seen him at the church. Like, is he as good and wholesome as he seems?"

"No one is completely wholesome, but he's the same man in private as he is in the pulpit. He shares his past with the congregation, warts and all."

"That takes balls for sure. I respect that."

Marci heard another creak in the floorboards. This time, Abel noticed it as well. She turned to him, unsure of what to say. He felt bad that his friend constantly felt the need to apologize for her modest home.

"Marci, it's alright. I use the same warped, rickety floor, remember? I live right next door."

"That board," she said, pointing across the room. "When the floor creaks right there, it tells me that... you're home."

They heard the floor creak again, this time accompanied by music coming through their shared wall. Abel instantly recognized it...

Bessie Smith sang "Baby Won't You Please Come Home." Abel quickly rose from the couch and headed for the door.

"Abe, wait!" Marci grabbed her purse and reached in for something. "Take this. You might need it."

Abel stepped out into the hallway, now filled with Bessie Smith coming from his apartment. He approached his door with Marci's small canister of pepper spray in hand, alarmed to see two spent matches at his feet, Carlos's trick further warning him that someone was inside. He stepped lightly as he slowly pushed his door open.

He entered his home carefully, looking around for anyone or anything, an easy task given the how bare his apartment was. He felt the ghostly presence of Regina, summoned by the music. She sat on the couch, her white gown delicately draped over her crossed legs as she held a glass of red wine and looked curiously at him. Abel ignored his late wife and scanned the studio.

Regina nodded to the bathroom just as Abel heard the toilet flush. With the pepper spray ready, he faced the door and was shocked to see a young girl emerge.

Livia Bellini, a 17-year-old brunette in jeans, sneakers, and baseball cap, stepped out of the bathroom and into range of Abel's wrath. Startled and quick to spot the pepper spray, she quickly raised both hands and squinted her eyes tight.

"Don't shoot!" Livia said with a yelp. "Don't... don't spray that shit on me!"

"Anyone else in there with you?"

"Yeah, I always take guests in the shitter when I gotta go!" Livia spoke with a working class Italian-American twang. "What the hell? No! Of course not!"

Abel took a quick peek into the bathroom. Satisfied that they were alone, he pocketed the pepper spray and walked to his desk. He shut off the turntable and turned to the couch, knowing his dead wife was gone.

"Talk," Abel said.

"Nice choice of music you got there, though you could offer more selection." She took a moment to study Abel's face, as if verifying that he was the man she'd been seeking.

"So you're him. It's an honor to meet... I mean... what I'm saying is... I heard about you."

"How unfortunate."

"Don't think it was easy! I mean, it's not like they talk about you at the corner store. You hear rumors, strange stories, you know? You start puttin' two and two. What I'm saying is no one sold you out or nothin'." She beamed with pride. "It was all detective work."

Abel shut the front door and braced it with a chair. He took off his coat and slung it over the second chair at the dining table. All the while, Livia remained at the bathroom doorway.

"Thanks for not freaking out on me," she said. "The door was unlocked, so I figured I'd wait. If you think about it, I was sorta house sitting, watching your stuff."

"Not much to watch."

"It beats living out of boxes, yeah?"

"Is that where you live?" Abel assumed his guest was simply a teenage girl living on the streets, looking for a vacant apartment to stay dry and warm.

"What? Me? No, I still live at home. I help my pop on the farm."

"You're telling me you're a farmer?"

"S'yeah. Kinda."

Abel quickly connected the dots. "And your two friends downstairs, are they kinda farmers as well?"

Livia stopped herself from answering too quickly, not wanting to overwhelm the man. Abel walked back his questioning, which started to feel like an interrogation, and started over by offering a handshake.

"My name is Abel Grant. I guess you already know that."

The girl slapped her palm to his and shook his hand firmly. "Livia Bellini. Those guys you're talking about, don't mind them. They watch over me is all. They're my muscle."

Abel walked to his refrigerator and pulled out a bottle of beer. He opened it with the palm of his hand and took a long drink in silence as Livia watched, still rooted at the bathroom door.

"Beer?" Abel asked. "It ain't much, but it's beer. Wait, can you even drink beer?"

Livia laughed and walked to the kitchen, taking a beer from the fridge. She failed to pop off the bottle cap with her bare hand like Abel did. Instead, she awkwardly took the unopened beer to the sofa and sat before her confused host.

"Detective Livia, why are you here?"

"My pop, he would never come to you himself. Mr. Big Shot is too proud. But he needs you."

"I work at the Royal Queen Motel. He can find me there during the day, but I guess you know that, too."

"I do, but I told ya, he's too proud." Livia struggled to open the bottle, but it didn't budge. "He won't come here. He don't even know I'm here now. Look, I know it's outside your zone, but I'm asking that you go to him. Go to the farm. I'm sure that if you show up, knock-knock on the door, he'll accept your help."

Abel took the beer bottle from Livia and popped it open for her, revealing the secret was the use of his wedding ring. He walked to the window overlooking the street.

"Outside my zone? There are no farms anywhere near the city."

"It's a drive, yeah. Two hours plus."

Abel's instincts told him to get rid of this audacious girl, to have her leave and visit him at the motel like everyone else, but the desperation in her eyes reminded him of his own torment, years before fleeing Texas for La Figueira. The girl wasn't there for herself. She traveled far to plead for his mercy on behalf of a loved one, a selfless act he couldn't easily dismiss. He worried about how she learned of his existence, but shelved that concern for the time being.

"Okay," Abel said with a sigh, unsure of what he was about to propose. "Give me a couple of days to take care of..."

"Thing is, it needs to happen soon, meaning tonight. Meaning now."

"Now? Why wait so long to ask?"

"Like I said, finding you wasn't easy."

Abel looked out the window, recognizing a man on the street below. He promptly made a call on his cell phone.

"Who you calling?" Livia asked, worried.

"Carlos?" Abel said on the phone. "What are you doing here?"

"Watching those guys," Carlos said from the sidewalk across the street. "I figured they might follow you home. Sure enough."

"I'm fine, Big Man."

"Can you speak freely? You alone?"

"I have a guest," Abel said, glancing at Livia on the sofa.

"What kind of guest? Want me to take care of him?"

"Go home, Carlos. I'll call if there's a need to 'take care' of anyone." Abel hung up and turned to Livia, who looked startled to hear his half of the grim conversation. "That was Carlos. He's my muscle."

"S'yeah. Good friends to have, huh?"

Abel read his guest for a moment, her pleading expression, her urgent tone, as he quickly weighed his choices.

"So, Abel Grant, where were we?" Livia asked, afraid of being shown the door.

"We were going to your farm."

\* \* \*

Far from the dark streets of the St. Nelia District, Livia's old pickup truck rumbled down a country four-laner in the foothills, her two bodyguards following in their sedan. Abel watched the city lights in the distance as Livia drove over ruts and potholes, nervously tapping the steering wheel.

"Pop don't trust outsiders," Livia said. "But I'll make him keep an open mind."

"How much farther?"

"We turn off the road ahead, then a short drive into Della Luna."

"Della Luna?" Abel asked, recognizing the name from his old life of enjoying the finer things. "As in Villaggio Della Luna? What kind of farm is this?"

As Livia thought of a response, they turned off the road and passed underneath a large wooden sign that spoke for her. "Bellini Family Wines" was spelled out in elegant letters across the overhead sign, welcoming visitors to what Abel could now see was a massive vineyard.

*Bellini.*

The name sounded familiar to Abel from the moment Livia introduced herself three hours before, but he hadn't connected it to the premium wines he had in the many white-tablecloth restaurants in Texas, and certainly not the "value wines" he saw in the countless liquor stores of St. Nelia.

Livia and her escort continued across the estate, down a long driveway lined with a white picket fences, until they reached a Colonial-style mansion of red brick and light gray trim. They parked near the grand entrance, between eight luxury sedans lined up in a row. Livia's old truck was the lone contrast. She shut off her engine, hopped out, and smiled at her bodyguards, pleased with herself for successfully bringing Abel there.

Abel stepped out of the truck, uneasy at the sight of the many cars. He took a look around the impressive property. "Quite a farm."

"I thought you might like it."

"I imagined a small farmhouse, cows and chickens, bales of hay, a rooster weathervane, maybe an apple pie cooling on a windowsill."

"Sorry to disappoint."

"It's fine," Abel said. "I've had my fill of pies."

Livia gestured a dismissal to her following guards. They remained at their car while she took Abel by the arm and led him onto the wrap-around porch and into the house.

"Livia, I normally help families of poverty, folks in dire need."

"Pop has money, sure, but he still needs your help. We need your help. That's why you came, yeah?"

They entered the opulent home and were immediately met by the stares of a dozen men in dress shirts and suits. They stood in an extravagant central hall at the foot of a wide staircase, their faces showing concern and apprehension. If Abel felt floored when he realized the farm was a vineyard, he was ever more puzzled to see tailored suits walking around in the middle of the night. He expected a nearly empty house and wondered again, this time to himself, "What kind of farm is this?"

"Check it out, Rigo!" Livia said. "Told ya I'd bring him!" She approached one of the men, the youngest in that hall.

Rodrigo "Rigo" Perez turned 30 that year but looked like he just graduated high school. He was tall, dark, and fit, well dressed and groomed like the others. Rigo spoke broken English with a thick Spanish accent. "Very good... your father... he will be please."

"Eh, I don't know about that, but he got no choice, yeah?"

Abel joined them, recognizing the young man's face from the day he healed his legs, and remembering his name from the day his cover was blown. "Hello again, Rigo. Your boss, Mr. Brennan, was just talking about you. He was right. You look better nowadays."

A few heads turned upon hearing "Brennan." Rigo ignored them, but felt the need to affirm his place.

"Brennan not my boss," Rigo said, making sure his associates heard him. "Not no more."

"Brennan stores our wines," Livia said, stepping between the two men. "Well, he used to. His company stored 'em and trucked 'em across the state. Rigo came on their last truck and never left." She smiled at her uncomfortable friend. "I guess we're stuck with him."

Abel noticed that Livia's nervous, awkward manner on display at his apartment was now gone. There, at the winery, she seemed relaxed and confident. She clearly had control over those men.

"How'd you know Brennan?" Livia asked.

"We sorta come from the same neighborhood."

Livia didn't seem to hear him as she walked to the foot of the stairs and peered up at the second floor. "Where's my pop?" she asked the group.

"In the room," Rigo said. "Praying the rosary."

"Go tell him to put that thing away. We're here now."

Rigo nodded and started up the stairs. Abel watched the young man's legs as he bounded up the steps two at a time. One would never know that he was once deemed crippled for life.

Livia stood on the third step of the grand staircase and addressed the men gathered in the hall. "Look at you all! I feel like I'm at a goddamn wake! You guys can go home. You'll get news when there's news to get. We got it from here."

The men looked at each other before hesitantly gathering their coats from nearby chairs that had been pulled into the hall from the adjacent dining room. They carried their chairs back to the long dinner table and made their way to the front door. Abel could feel their stares of uncertainty as they passed him on their way out.

Livia waited until the last associate was gone before taking Abel further into the house. She again grabbed his arm and guided him down the hall to an ornate office. A large oak desk sat alongside a wine rack that spanned an entire wall. Across from the hundreds of resting wine bottles sat a wet bar under a painting of the vineyard at sunrise.

"I can't guarantee we got that swill you call beer," Livia said, "but we got lots of other stuff. Pop demands the best."

"I can see. But not now, thank you. Were those men your employees?"

"Some," Livia said. "Some are cousins, some are friends, and some are paycheck players. But yeah, I suppose they all work for us."

"They're concerned for your mother? Is that why they were here so late?"

"Some," Livia said again. "Some are concerned. Some were here just 'cause they're expected to be."

"Do you trust these men?" Abel asked.

Livia hesitated to answer, which she knew was its own answer.

"Let me guess," Abel said. "Some."

"Yeah."

"That's not good enough, Livia. You know I'm a private person. If you don't trust them all, I can't trust you."

"Some I trust because they're good guys. They like us. They're loyal. The rest, I trust 'cause they get a good paycheck. So, yeah, I'll go on record and say I trust them all."

"Fair enough," Abel said, though his unease grew by the minute. He worried that perhaps there was no gravely ill mother, no emergency, that it was an elaborate ploy to lure him to Della Luna, caught in a trap without Carlos at nearly 3:00 a.m. Memories of Texas suddenly came into focus.

Either way, he needed to go upstairs to the woman's bedroom immediately. He realized she indeed existed because he suddenly felt her pain, a long endured torment on the second floor. "Your father's up there? With your mother?"

"Pop? Yeah, he prays with her, even when she's out for the night. Doctor gave her some pills that knock her out cold. It's the only way she can sleep." She and Abel turned toward the sound of approaching footsteps on the carpeted staircase, soon coming down the hall.

David Bellini entered the office, a man of 60 in a dress shirt, boots, and suspenders. He served as the patriarch of both his family and the estate. Rosary beads dangled from his left hand while he scratched his full gray beard with his right. He scrutinized his mysterious guest as if he were the one about to spring a trap.

"You must be the king of this beautiful castle," Abel said with a smile, breaking the tense silence. He approached David in front of the wine rack wall and offered a handshake. "My name is Abel Grant."

With eyes locked, David shook Abel's hand a few seconds too long, enough to make him uncomfortable. He spoke firmly and to the point, often interrupting what he deemed "superfluous chit-chat." Livia had hoped he'd soften in the presence of the man they desperately needed, but she knew better.

"David Bellini," he said, introducing himself at the end of the handshake. "And I already know who you are. My daughter's been talking you up for weeks. I should put her on my sales team."

"Mr. Bellini..."

"David."

"David," Abel said, correcting himself with a grin. "I don't normally make house calls, but as you pointed out, Livia can be persuasive."

David looked at his daughter, who suddenly seemed withdrawn. "And what did my persuasive princess tell you?"

"That your wife is quite ill..."

"Cancer."

Abel noted David's abrupt tone, his impatience, and threw away the usual formalities. He needed to let David lead their conversations, as it would be the only way to connect with the man. "How long?"

"Almost a year." David waited for more ceremony, more nonsense courtesy to lower his guard, but his guest remained silent. Now David felt uncomfortable. He took control of their exchange, as he was accustomed to. "Forgive my manners, we can discuss this later. Are you tired from the drive? Something to eat? We have plenty of good wine."

"Perhaps later. Is your wife awake..."

"Rosemary. She's asleep, thank The Lord. The pain builds across the day. I used to hate her snoring, but now it's a blessing to hear it."

"Like a buzzsaw!" Livia said. "Right, pop?"

David gave his daughter a stern look, forcing her smile to drop.

"It's late," David said. "Livia will prepare the guest house for you, Mr. Grant." Livia took the passive command as her cue to leave. David waited for her footsteps to reach the end of the hall before continuing. "Forgive her for being brash.

It's my fault for raising her like a son. My first wife said I should have given her a rag doll. Instead, I gave her a hunting rifle."

David sat behind his desk and picked up a decanter of wine that had been waiting for him. He poured two glasses and handed one to Abel as he took the seat across from him.

"La Donna Tempesta," David said with pride, holding his quarter-filled glass to the light with a swirl. He watched as Abel took his first sip and could tell he was impressed. "Good. I can see you know quality. 1999, the dawn of a new millennium. Harvest came after a storm. The vines fought to survive. Steepest part of the hill, away from the sun. Makes the berries rich with flavor. You must make them suffer to make them sublime. It's my most cherished vintage."

"Indeed, it's exquisite, but shouldn't we talk about your wife..."

"Rosemary. Either you can or can't help. There's nothing else to discuss. And wine always comes first when talking business here."

"This is not business," Abel said pointedly. "I'm not here for money."

David ignored his guest's urgency. He sipped his wine, savoring the delicate vintage.

"I should see Rosemary right away," Abel said. "Mr. Bellini..."

"David."

"David." Abel grew tired of his host's need to steer every moment. It might have been costing his wife precious time. "You don't seem like a man who calls in men like me."

"What kind of man do I seem like?"

"Like the kind of man who has money. Surely, you have a good doctor."

"Dr. Flowers," David said. "She's the best."

"Livia says you demand that."

David picked up the decanter. He rose to his feet, sat on the edge of his desk in front of Abel, and refilled both of their glasses. "Let me tell you the kind of man I am, Mr. Grant. I'm the kind who does whatever it takes. Were you my first choice? No. God is always with us in these hills. I could ask nothing more." He walked to the open door and looked in the hall to see if anyone was listening before returning to his desk. "But I've heard stories about you, from those who would not share them easily, no-nonsense men who earned my respect. And, of course, there's my persuasive princess. She's convinced of your... gift."

Abel felt Rosemary's pain rise, as if begging him to head upstairs. Like his host moments before, he now needed to dispense with civility and shot straight to the point. "Thank you again for the wine, but I insist, I must see her right away."

"And why is that?" David asked.

"Because I can't heal the dead."

On that striking, grim note, Livia returned and poked her head into the office.

"She's waking up!"

\* \* \*

The master bedroom of the Bellini estate dwarfed even the most robust suburban home. Huge, round skylights in the ceiling two stories above let in the stars, untouched by the light pollution that blinded La Figueira's night sky. Abel gazed up at the skylights as if someone was looking down at him, waiting to see what he'd do next. He'd been raised to believe that God always watched over him, but given the events of the past ten years, Abel couldn't conclude if He protected him or merely observed, as if the days of his life played on a celestial television.

Colossal in both size and luxury, the room housed surprisingly few items. An antique vanity sat against the north wall near the bathroom. A pair of bureaus sat on the south wall, a walk-in closet between them. On the west wall, directly across from the door, a four-poster king-size bed draped in floral sheets and topped with down pillows held the slender frame of Rosemary Bellini, her sleeping face lit by a single Virgin Mary candle atop a bedside table. She wore white satin gloves to discourage her from scratching her many sores and tumors. They were hidden from view, though Abel felt them all.

Abel stood at the foot of the bed with Livia and David, for that was as far as David would allow until his wife had awakened.

"Mr. Grant," David said, "if you see me as the king of this castle, allow me to present my queen."

Abel considered her a timeless beauty, her motherhood and 45 years barely lining her peaceful expression. As Abel's eyes adjusted to the low light of the room, he realized Rosemary wore a black kerchief around her head, failing to hide the fact that she had become bald from rounds of intense chemotherapy that ultimately did nothing to deter her cancer. The disease started in her left breast but quickly fanned out through her torso like a massive hand. Unlike with others he'd helped, Abel didn't need to be told the extent of her plight. He could feel it the moment he entered the dark bedroom.

Rosemary opened her eyes, her tilted head facing her toward the candle flame. David approached her, kneeling down to talk with her, but silenced himself when his wife struggled to speak. Her voice sounded faint, weak, yet still distinct.

"David," Rosemary said. "Did you eat?"

"Oh yes, very well. Rose, someone's here to see you."

"Dr. Flowers?"

"No, Rose. She's coming tomorrow, but there's a man here now who comes highly recommended."

Rosemary pointed a finger at the two bedside tables flanking her. Livia knew she wanted more candles lit. The light switch on the wall hadn't been used for months, the room's inset lights proving too harsh for her mother's eyes.

As a few more candles lit the room, Abel stepped forward into view, his knees nearly touching the footboard. Rosemary addressed him in her soft voice, belying a cynical tone.

"You're the 'angel' I've heard about."

"Word gets around."

"My stepdaughter gets around. You're here to fix me, then?"

"I'm here to try."

"Try? You don't offer The Lord as your personal guarantee? I'll have you know I don't believe in false prophets."

"I don't believe in prophets either," Abel said. "False or otherwise. But here I am." Abel turned to David and Livia standing near the Virgin Mary candle. "Whatever happens, do not intervene."

David nodded that he understood, even if he didn't yet believe any of this. He led his daughter aside, near the vanity, as Abel took their place at Rosemary's side. He sat on the bed and held her left hand, encased in a satin glove.

"I asked you about The Lord," she said. "What does He do with a sinner like me? What does He do while I lay here and wonder?"

"Wonder?" Abel asked, trying to dull the edge of his defiant attitude. "Do you wonder if He loves you? If he cares at all? If your years of faith and devotion meant anything? Believe me, I understand your doubt."

"I don't doubt any of that, Mr. Grant. Every time I feel myself drifting asleep, I wonder if I'll wake. Every time I see David's face, or Livia's, I wonder if it will be the last time. When the sunrise comes in through the windows, I wonder if I'll ever see another. So, I ask you again, what does The Lord do with a sinner like me?"

"I can't speak for Him. No one can, not even the highest of the mighty."

Rosemary let out a little laugh, which turned into a coarse cough. "And you would have me to believe you're His Hand?" She breathed deep through dense lungs.

"I can tell you He watches and listens, but that He only does two things that we can see."

"And what are those?"

"The Lord giveth and The Lord taketh away."

Abel slid the long glove off her arm and placed his palm to hers. Without having to search for it as he often did, he was immediately struck with the feeling. He quickly clutched her hand with both of his and shut his eyes.

Livia looked concerned, not expecting the suspense and fear of anticipating a miraculous act. She grabbed her father's hand, a gesture that felt premature to him. He still awaited results, still saw such grand ceremony as likely a charlatan's gimmick, the dramatic gestures of a carnival mentalist at work.

Abel paused and opened his eyes, still locked hand-in-hand with Rosemary, and scanned her body as if searching for every trace of the cancer. He clinched his eyes again, wincing from a sudden wave of pain. Rosemary craned her back and fell to the bed once more, laying still as if about to drift asleep, an agonizing sight David couldn't bear to witness.

"That's quite enough!" David said.

Livia tugged at her father's arm and looked him square in the eye, begging him to stay calm.

Abel finally released Rosemary and stood up from the bed. He trudged to the bathroom, past the vanity, behind David and Livia. As soon as Abel stepped through the doorway, David heard him collapse to the tile floor and cough up what sounded like a quart of vomit into the toilet. David nodded for Livia to tend to their guest while he checked on his wife.

David offered to help Rosemary sit up in bed, but she didn't need assistance. She sat on her own, breathed deeply, and smiled at him. They looked at each other in amazement.

\* \* \*

Four hours later, the sun rose over Della Luna's steep hills lined with thousands of vines, a beautiful sight Abel failed to see. Though the guest house at the rear of the property had been prepared for him, he couldn't even muster the strength to make it down the stairs. Livia guided him to a Victorian couch in the second-floor hall just outside her parents' room and was shocked and saddened to see him pass out the second his head rested on a velvet cushion. She brought him a pitcher of water and a plate of apple slices, but made no attempt to speak with him or wake him, following his strict order not to intervene. Instead, she plopped into a chair across the hall, sure to be near in case he needed her.

When Livia woke along with the sun, she saw the water and the apples, but no sign of the angel. She ran down the stairs in search of him, imagining the worst. Her first instinct was to find her father.

Abel sat on the lowered tailgate of Livia's truck parked in front of the house. With the sun shining and the many sedans gone, the property appeared more spacious and manicured than he remembered from the night before. He smoked a cigarette and watched a flock of finches in a nearby tree as he patiently waited to be taken home.

David and Livia emerged from the house, relieved to see Abel seemed well after his short rest. David halted his daughter at the porch, scratching his head in thought.

"Dr. Flowers needs to do some tests to be sure," he said.

"We don't need no tests, Pop. Mama's all turned around now."

"Your 'angel' exploited her faith, convinced her of a miracle. She was desperate enough to buy it. It doesn't mean she's out of the woods."

Livia stared at her father, incredulous. "She straight up told him 'Fuck off, false prophet!' She didn't buy into him no more than you."

"She certainly does now," David said, stubbornly refusing to accept his wife's apparent recovery as a divine act. "There's a sucker born every minute. In this house, there were two minutes."

"He did it, Pop! He did something your money and men couldn't do! And you're too pig-headed to see it!"

David slapped Livia hard across the face, an impulse he instantly regretted, though he'd never dare show it. From the truck, Abel turned toward the sharp sound. Both men saw David hadn't hurt Livia so much as angered her. She stomped back into the house.

Curious, Abel snuffed his cigarette into the gravel driveway and joined his host on the porch. "Normally, this is the part where folks hug and kiss and cry."

"And tell you how grateful they are and call you God's Hand on Earth. They offer money, but you refuse, keeping their debt in your pocket to do with as you please."

"There are no debts to me, Mr..."

"David."

"David. I don't work for money. I thought I made that clear when we met."

"You think a fool built this place?" David gestured his open arms to his grand manor. "You think you're the first shaman to be brought here by my wide-eyed child? I humor her, pay for her 'healers,' thank them for a nice try, better luck next time, then send them on their way. But that little theatre you put on is more sinister. You've got your claws in them now, but The Lord will see you burn for toying with my family."

"The Lord's done enough," Abel said. "And invoking His name to threaten me is not only offensive, but futile. I've been burning for nine years."

Before David could unpack Abel's loaded retort, Livia returned and shoved a white handkerchief in her father's left hand. Without warning, she grabbed his right hand, revealed a steak knife, and viciously slashed his palm with the serrated blade. David cursed from the shock of it, stepped back as blood plopped onto the porch.

Facing the men's stunned expressions, she dropped the knife and barked a command at Abel.

"Do it!"

Abel instantly knew what she had in mind. He hesitated, even as he felt the sting of David's wound. "I'm not a monkey to perform on demand. I help people. No games, no converting non-believers. Your father made himself quite clear." He readied another cigarette, but Livia snatched it from him.

"Do it!" she screamed again, her desperate voice breaking on the verge of tears.

Abel took out another cigarette, lit it, and took a long drag as he watched the finches in their simple life among the trees. He looked down at the tickle of blood passing between his feet and laughed at what he saw as another moment of 'theater' her father would surely mock.

David took him by the arm and offered his own command as a calm request. "You heard my daughter. Show her what she wants to see, oh shaman."

Abel took another drag, flung his cigarette into the driveway, and turned toward David. He held David's wound like a simple handshake. Unlike last night's torment, there was no kneeling, no anguished expressions, just two men facing each other on the porch, hand-in-hand.

David felt something strange, a tingling sensation in his palm that traveled up his arm and into his chest. He tried to yank his hand away but found it locked in that bloody grip, as if fused to the man. Abel stared at him until he calmed down and stopped resisting. A few seconds later, Abel released him.

Dr. Amy Flowers, a middle-aged woman in a quarter-length coat, emerged from the house carrying her medical bag. Oblivious to the tension, she smiled at the three people standing in a circle before noticing the spatter of blood at their feet. Her eyes darted up to David's red soaked sleeve.

"What happened here?" Dr. Flowers asked. "David, are you hurt?"

David raised his hand to his face, realizing that the burning pain had passed. He wiped the blood from his palm with the handkerchief and saw that the deep cut was gone, with no trace of injury and no scar to show for it. He looked up at Dr. Flowers, barely able to get the words out.

"I'm fine, Doctor," David said.

"Let me have a look." Dr. Flowers examined David's hand. There was plenty of blood but no cut.

"Enough about me," David said, snapping out of his awe. "How is Rosemary?"

"Rose? She's a new woman! I'm not exactly sure what happened. Maybe it's all this fresh, clean air, but her lungs are clear. Even the protrusions on her neck and chest have disappeared."

"Thank you, Doctor. You've always been attentive to Rose. I want you to know I appreciate the long hours you've spent here, all the overnight stays."

Dr. Flowers sensed a farewell in his tone. "David, I still need to check for any biomarkers before I can..."

"How long before the tests?"

"Tomorrow. Maybe today. I'll push them in the lab. I'm definitely interested in seeing the results myself."

"Then, please, get to it."

Confused, Dr. Flowers had nothing more to add. She walked to her car, started the engine, and drove off down the long, gravel driveway, leaving David to wonder about his new hand. He moved it around, quietly amazed.

"Ten seconds," David said in a near whisper. "Just ten seconds, and it was nothing to you."

"Not like last night," Livia said.

"Big difference between a simple cut and years of ravaging cancer." Abel wiped his hand on the handkerchief as best he could.

"I don't even feel my arthritis anymore," David said.

"I'm guessing you only had that for a year or so."

"That's right."

"Livia? Shall we go?" Abel nodded to her pickup truck.

David moved both hands, made fists, stretched his fingers, feeling as if he'd been given a younger man's arms. He looked at his guest with new eyes. "Please, stay a while, Mr. Grant."

"What my pop is saying is, 'Sorry for doubting you, Mr. Grant, sir,'" Livia said pointedly.

Abel opened the passenger door of the truck. "I'm afraid I can't stay..."

"You must," David said. "That's my payment to you. Something I made. My home. My hospitality. You are my guest. And Livia is right, Mr. Grant, as blunt as she is. I'm sorry for my doubt."

"Actually, you paid me in advance. You shared your finest wine with me last night. We're good."

"But not good enough. You must stay and allow me to make up for my crass behavior. Please, I insist."

Abel considered his simple offer and nodded that he would remain a while longer. Without another word, David headed back into the house, still stunned.

Livia crossed her arms and looked at Abel with a wide grin across her face. "Buddy, you've got my pop like no one else ever has."

"How's that?"

"He's in your debt. He hates that. But he always pays his debts."

"There are no debts to me."

"S'yeah. Good luck telling him that."

*  *  *

Carlos felt unnerved, alone at the Royal Queen Motel. He paced in front his office window, checking the time on his watch every thirty seconds. His cell phone vibrated and rang, and his hand ran into his pocket to answer it.

"Boss?"

"Good morning, Carlos."

"Dammit, man, where you at?"

"Villaggio Della Luna."

"Villa... what?"

"I'm at a vineyard up north in the coastal hills."

"Shit, of all the places you coulda been, I never woulda guessed that."

"Neither would I, but I'm fine."

The wineries of the California Central Coast felt like another planet to Carlos. He never thought much about that decadent world, especially since committing to Abel and The Mission, but he suddenly saw it as a fortress holding his boss captive. "You comin' back or what?"

"Yes, but for now, hold off on our appointments. You know what to tell them."

Carlos didn't like cancelling an entire day so suddenly. He knew Abel wouldn't turn away visitors unless he was in trouble. "Sure, but you want me to come out there? To Della-Whatever?"

"Not yet, Big Man. Wine country doesn't suit you. I know it doesn't suit me. I'll be here for the day."

"You for sure about this? I mean, who are these people? And there ain't nothing you want me to do?"

Abel thought about how Livia had found him, how she entered his apartment without incident. "Can you fix my apartment door?"

"Boss, you know I can fix anything."

"Do that for me. I'll keep in touch."

Abel hung up, leaving Carlos to face six desperate people with bad news. He calmed himself and returned to his office, hoping that Abel would call him back soon.

# 6

## Scars

The morning sun shone through the stained glass windows high on the chapel's east wall of The Community United Church of the Beloved St. Nelia. A few dozen people sat scattered in the pews, tired, desperate, some hungover, some smelling of alcohol drank only minutes before entering the early service. They watched Reverend Dean walk up to his pulpit, Bible in hand, his sermon tucked within its pages. He looked about the room as if happy to see old friends. As always, he wore simple blue jeans underneath his black clergy shirt and collar, affectionately referring to them as his "carpenter jeans" in honor of Jesus.

"Good morning, Family," he said into the microphone mounted to his pulpit. His calm voice could be heard clearly in every corner of the large chapel, coming from small speakers mounted on the walls every fifteen feet.

The group respectfully replied, "Good morning" nearly in unison, their voices faint, not yet fully awake. Despite the reverend's greeting, there were no families in attendance, only hardened adults living hard lives. They sat gathered for a weekly dose of "Face Your Demons," a special service meant for those who struggled on the streets.

"This morning at breakfast, a young man was shivering, not from the cold, but from withdrawals. He's not living, Family, he's surviving. He asked me, 'What's the point of all this, Reverend? What's the point of life?' Six a.m. and already I get hit with the tough questions."

The group laughed, more at the reverend's goofy grin than his little punchline. More folks entered, and he turned to them walking in through the chapel's open double doors. As he continued his sermon, he pointed them to vacant seats along the central aisle.

"Six a.m. I was barely awake, hadn't had my coffee yet, but I had an answer for that young man. Life is about choices. How you treat a neighbor. How you speak to a friend. How you welcome a stranger. How you see yourself. Always remember, Family, how you treat one another is essentially how you regard God because He is within each of us. He connects us."

Arlo sat in the front row, entranced by the sermon. The stocky roughneck looked awkward in his tight-fitting dress shirt and necktie, his massive arms barely squeezed into their sleeves. By the time he got to the boxes of donated clothes the day before, the selection had dwindled. Rather than feel frustrated, he felt lucky to have found anything worthy of one of the reverend's special sermons, even if it did cling to him two sizes too small.

"This group is special," Reverend Dean said, looking into everyone's eyes. "You hold a place in my heart because you're not here simply for weekly worship. Each of you have an uphill battle. You're here to... Face! Your! Demons!"

The group applauded with spirit and enthusiasm. Arlo clapped the loudest, barely containing his emotions.

"For those who don't break, that uphill climb strengthens you. Let the demons squeeze your lump of coal hard enough, it reveals the diamond underneath. You suffer so that you may shine, and so we face our demons, and we thank them."

The group says "Thank you, demons," a routine response to Reverend Dean's unusual sermon. Arlo shut his eyes tight and nodded as he recited the response, inspired, rocking in his seat.

"The good news, Family, is that you don't have to face them alone. Who needs a copy of our program?"

Several hands went up. Arlo stood with a stack of pamphlets and handed them out.

"This gentle giant is Arlo Rosewood. He's the man to see if you want to join a workshop or schedule a private session with me. He's all over this church, hard at work every day, so get used to seeing his pretty face a lot."

The group laughed again. Arlo smirked at the playful jab as he took a seat in the back row, eager to reconnect with the reverend.

Beside him sat Carlos, seemingly unmoved by the service.

"Some of you know me. For those who don't, the first thing I'll tell you, even before my name, is that my folks raised me to be a good Catholic boy. But like many of you, I hurt others. As a child, I was a bully and an ingrate. As a young man, I killed people in their homeland for my Uncle Sam. Later, I neglected my wife, turned away my son, mistreated my friends. Hurting them, I also hurt myself. When I crawled out of a bar at dawn for the last time, when I reacquainted myself with The Lord, the first thing He taught me is that you share the scars of those you wound, and oh, so many scars have I."

The group nodded in sympathy. Most of them knew his history well, and all of them had lived their version of it.

"I remind myself of that lesson every day - when we hurt others, we hurt ourselves. But there's another side to that coin, Family. In helping others, we help ourselves. The scars never go away, but they can represent all the healing you've done. The demons never go away, but they can watch as you defy them with your kindness and compassion. Now, I ask you to call out any saints you wish to be named so that they may watch over us all. Let us bow our heads."

Everyone lowered their heads in prayer except Carlos. Reverend Dean noticed the large gangster, feeling his eyes upon him.

"Saint Martin," said a man in the third row.

"Saint Martin, watch over us," Reverend Dean said, his hands raised in praise.

"Saint Augustine," said a woman in the ninth row.

"Saint Augustine, watch over us."

"*Saint Abel*," Carlos shouted, his voice piercing the room.

Reverend Dean stared at him, tried to read him from across the chapel. "Saint Abel, watch over us."

* * *

After the "Face Your Demons" service ended, Arlo stepped outside to schedule workshops, classes, and private counseling. He shook hands with each member of the flock, welcoming new folks to the congregation and encouraging them to attend the following week's sermon. From the corner of his eye, he watched Reverend Dean hug Carlos and lead him to his office.

Once inside, the reverend shut the door and gestured for Carlos to have a seat. To the gangster's surprise, the reverend remained standing, troubled, bracing himself for bad news.

"Is 'Saint Abel' in trouble?" Reverend Dean asked.

"He's in Della Luna, two hours out in the wine country. Couple of guys took him there last night. You know who David Bellini is?"

Reverend Dean did indeed know that name, just as he also knew Brennan.

"You swore you'd keep him safe!" the reverend said. "You swore to me and you swore to God!"

"Hey, I tailed those assholes all day..."

"Watch your language in this house."

"Fuck your language rule!" Carlos said. "There's more important things to focus on right now, and of all the people in this shitty world, you should know better than to attack my devotion, reverend."

Reverend Dean thought about Carlos's past, how he came to commit himself to Abel's mission. "I'm sorry, son. I don't question your faith. Simple respect is all I ask for in this church. Now, about these men…"

"Like I said, I tailed them for hours, but Abel said it was cool."

"And you believed him?"

"I believe in him."

"That's a different matter, and you know it. Abel's put himself in harm's way before." Reverend Dean brushed past his friend and made a call on his desk phone. "If everything is 'cool,' Carlos, why are you here?" After hearing three rings, he hung up the phone, unsure.

"I'm here 'cause he's still out there."

Reverend Dean looked at his wall of photos, at Abel sitting in a dunk tank at a fundraiser carnival. "Bellini, you say?"

"David Bellini, yeah. So what do we do?"

"Right now, all we can do is trust him, wait, and pray. Just keep me posted."

Carlos seemed ever more concerned as Reverend Dean opened the door for him to leave. Frustrated, the former gangster stood and headed out. "It's fuckin' Texas Goldie all over again," he muttered as he approached the doorway.

To Carlos's shock, Reverend Dean quickly shut the door before his friend could leave, putting things together for the first time. "Texas Goldie? He didn't work with that con man, Pastor Reeves, did he?"

"Yeah, that's the guy. Abel never told you?"

"Not a word. All I know is he served a flock in Texas before coming here, and that things went badly for you boys."

"It wasn't our finest hour," Carlos said. "That's how he puts it."

"What happened?"

"Shit hit the shit. It's why we came here, back to my old hood. That's all I got to say."

Reverend Dean recalled the strange, final appearance of the infamous Pastor Reeves in Texas. It never occurred to him that Abel and Carlos were present that day. "I read about it in the paper. You were actually there? Working for Reeves?"

Carlos reached for the doorknob, determined to let his boss tell their regrettable tale once he returned to St. Nelia. Instead, to the reverend's relief, he returned to his seat in front of the desk.

"I been with him before that," Carlos said. "I always been with him."

* * *

During the second week of December in 2011, nearly ten years before moving to the St. Nelia District of La Figueira, Carlos's first day serving Abel took place not at a church nor abandoned motel but at Grant's Blues Joint, an upscale nightclub in the heart of Austin, Texas. The club was closed during the day, allowing Abel time to stock and clean the bar to prepare for a busy evening. He rarely employed staff for prep time, usually enjoying the work alone. Considering it was the club's final month, he'd spent every afternoon setting up without help. He wanted to savor every detail of his beloved club before shutting its doors for the last time.

Carlos and five other members of the Lincoln Heights Guerreros entered the club, looking around at the art deco decor. Abel had popped the door open to help dry the floors after a quick mop. Upon seeing the men come in, he felt startled and cautious, but soon relieved upon seeing Carlos among them.

"See, told ya we found him," one of the gangsters said to Carlos. No other words were spoken as the men took turns hugging their former lieutenant before stepping out and shutting the door, leaving Carlos alone with the man they'd spent weeks searching for. He approached Abel at the bar.

"My boys said you ran a club," Carlos said. "I didn't believe them."

"What did you expect?"

"I dunno, something more... holy."

"Me, too. I felt two callings early in life, but music had a stronger pull."

"Don't get me wrong, man, this place is nice. I drove by a dozen times since we been here, never thought of walking in. A blues bar just ain't my thing."

"We're all blues fans sooner or later because we all get that feeling."

"What feeling?"

"The feeling that the world has done us wrong, that all hope is gone, and all we have left is to express it with our art, our music, our voices. We've all been there, Big Man, and we call it the blues."

"I suppose so," Carlos said. "Never looked at it like that."

As Abel continued to prepare for the evening, Carlos took down a barstool and sat as if the evening's first patron. He spotted a framed photo on the wall - Abel and Regina posed in a designer suit and sparkling evening dress, with Abel behind a grand piano and Regina sitting atop it, holding a microphone.

"That your wife?" Carlos asked. "Damn, she's fine as hell. She the star of this place?"

"Absolutely," Abel said with a smile.

"And you look like Duke Ellington sittin' at that piano. You any good?"

"You're familiar with The Duke? I'm impressed." Abel pulled up his right sleeve, revealing a web of ragged scars across his wrist and palm. "Oh, I was good alright. I was real good... until the night you and I met."

Carlos turned away from the grim memory. He noticed an impressive sketch framed on the wall by the bar, an angel drawn in the style of graffiti, the same picture that would adorn Abel's apartment wall for years to come.

"You actually hung it up," Carlos said.

"It's art, isn't it?"

"I just... I never seen my shit framed on a wall. Makes it look all legit."

"You have talent," Abel said. "You're as legit as they come. How's your arm?"

"Brand new. I done 'H' five-hundred times and even those tracks are gone. It's like I never shot the shit. Don't want it no more."

"You're welcome."

Abel opened a bottle of beer and set it in front of his guest. "Where'd your friends go? I'll buy 'em a few rounds."

"Ain't my friends no more. Maybe that means they never was. Them finding you, takin' me here, that was my big goodbye."

Abel looked at him as if to ask why, but it proved difficult for Carlos to elaborate. He spoke slowly as he relived their shared memory.

"That night we met," Carlos said. "I killed four good people."

"You weren't responsible for all four..."

"FOUR good people. My old friends and my nephew. He was barely fifteen, wasn't no gang-banger, you know? Now he ain't nothing. It shoulda been me."

"I know the feeling."

"So I said I'm outta there, I'm outta the Guerreros, and nobody said shit to stop me. Maybe that's respect, or maybe that's them getting rid of bad luck."

"They're not following you anymore?"

"No," Carlos said. "'Cause from now on I'm following you."

Carlos felt nervous about his proclamation. He'd rehearsed a well-worded plea but abandoned it, simply stating his intention and waiting for a response. He looked at Abel, hoping he wouldn't turn him away. The reformed criminal had just slammed the door on his old life and desperately sought a new one.

Abel took glassware out of the dishwasher as he processed Carlos's commitment.

"This club is nice," Carlo said. "What a life you got."

"I thought it was my life. The club. The music. I poured everything into it. Turns out she was my life."

Carlos hated hearing that, the words stinging him like barbed wire pulled tight around his heart. He looked down in shame.

"I'm closing the club this weekend," Abel said. "After driving by a dozen times, you're lucky you came while you still could."

Carlos stood and walked up to his framed drawing. "Why'd you ask me for this? I put twenty-grand in your hand, every buck I had, but you turned it down, said to draw you something instead."

"I saw artwork in the car. Somehow, I knew it was yours, knew that was the payment, not any amount of money."

"Why?"

Abel stopped stocking glasses for a moment, not sure how to explain his unusual request. "There are tribes in Africa that predate all the world's nations. When their medicine men heal someone, there has to be an exchange, a trade for something made or grown. It's balance. Without it, the miracle may come undone. A trade makes it 'legit.' Just a tradition, that's all."

Abel checked the time on his watch. He went to the front door and opened it for the evening. Carlos followed him. "You're not leaving, are you Big Man? Gonna be a hell of a night."

"I ain't never leaving you, Boss."

*Boss.*

Abel again considered the proposal for a moment. He looked into Carlos's pleading eyes. "In that case, fill the ice bins. Candles and flowers on every table. Arrange them however you want, just make them look nice."

Carlos obeyed the command without a second thought, hurrying behind the bar. As he refilled the ice, he turned to his new boss. "If this place is shuttin' down, where we going next?"

"You watch TV? You heard of Pastor Goldie Reeves?" Carlos nodded, confused. "God put our lives in ruin. The way I see it, we might as well get something out of this mess."

Carlos didn't understand what Abel meant, didn't grasp his blasphemy, but accepted the next chapter of his life.

# 7

# Pitchfork

There were two dining rooms at Bellini Family Wines. The first took up the newly built east wing of the house, resembling an indoor-outdoor banquet hall, serving tourists during the summer months. They enjoyed mid-range wines, local cuisine, and light entertainment. The second dining room rested along the west wing between the rear patio and swimming pool, serving only the Bellinis and their guests. This private room saw only the estate's best, reserved wines and gourmet meals by the family's personal chef.

Abel sat at the long, well-appointed table, opposite Rosemary who had handpicked the evening's menu in honor of the angel who saved her life. Two servants entered and poured them each a glass of red wine, the grand dinner yet to be served. Rosemary held her wine to the light, swirled it, and took in its aroma before nodding approval to her staff. Only then did they leave the room.

"I assume you picked the wine," Abel said.

"I always do. David will be the first to tell you that my tastebuds trump even his."

"So, why did your staff wait for your approval just now?"

"Even the best wines can go bad. Improper storage, cork rot, flaws in the bottling. Tourists drink their wine right after the pour, paying no mind to the delicate details. To truly taste wine, you must inspect it first, test it with your eyes and nose before it touches your palate."

"Show me." Abel asked for the demonstration if only to kill time until the rest of the family arrived. It felt awkward to simply stare at each other across the vast table. He picked up his glass and followed her example.

"You must hold it to the light to look for particulates," she said, swirling her glass just above eye level. "Also note the color. Brown is bad. It means the wine is over the hill." She tilted the glass and stuck her nose into its bulb, taking several quick sniffs. "Next, observe its nose. Watch out for off scents of mold, vinegar, heavy raisin."

"When do we actually take a sip?"

"Right now." They each took a sip of wine, Rosemary puckering her lips to suck in a little air, making a slurping sound. "You're looking for flavors of fruit, wood, herbs. If it tastes astringent or chemical, throw it out. Not only will it fail to impress, but it could get you sick. It's the difference between feeling fuzzy the next morning versus wrestling with a clobbering hangover."

Abel laughed at Rosemary's tone, a proper tutorial that sounded nearly self-mocking, like parody. Though the woman took her wine seriously, she clearly knew how pompous it all seemed.

Livia entered, trying not to seem hurried, and sat beside her stepmother. She smiled at their little wine tasting lesson as she poured herself a glass and immediately downed it in a single gulp. Rosemary seemed frustrated with her, not for her lack of poise, but her tardiness.

"Now, we can finally eat," Rosemary said, waving to her servants on standby in the adjacent kitchen. They promptly served a lavish meal of Salmon Tartare, Camembert Fondue, White Gazpacho Soup, Coq Au Vin, and Roast Rack of Lamb. Abel hadn't eaten so well in years, accustomed to greasy empanadas and dry tamales on his best nights.

"Sorry for being late," Livia said. She tore a dinner roll in half and dipped it in the fondue. "Had to wash up. I was deep in the field."

"We have field workers for that."

"You want me to learn the family business, yeah? It means gettin' dirty."

"Shouldn't we wait for David?" Abel asked, alone on his side of the table.

"He eats at his desk during harvest," Rosemary said.

"Pop calls it a 'working dinner.'"

Abel only took one bite of his salmon before quick footsteps were heard coming down the hall. Rigo entered a panic, out of breath, barely able to get his words out.

"We need the angel!"

* * *

Rigo drove a small, blue farm utility vehicle with large off-road tires down a meandering dirt trail, taking Abel out into the fields under an overcast night sky. The trail weaved through endless rows of vines, the mansion now far behind them. Having only seen the fields leading up to the house, Abel couldn't believe the immense size of the rear property, stretching up into the steep hills as far as he could see.

They stopped in front of a rickety bunkhouse, barely standing, a relic from the winery's founding 91 years before. A short distance away stood the picturesque Colonial guest house that had been prepared for Abel's stay.

Rigo and Abel hopped out of the utility vehicle and entered the long, narrow bunkhouse. Rows of beds lined the walls. Work clothes and tools hung from nails hammered into the headboards. A dozen Mexican field workers in dirty denim overalls and stained cotton shirts stood gathered around a bed near the center of the room.

"His name Miguel," Rigo said in his broken English as they approached the workers. "Let me know... if need help."

Rigo spoke to the group in Spanish, explaining that Abel had come to take care of the fallen man, ordering them to give him room to perform his miracle. Though Abel understood Rigo's command and his over-the-top description of the scene, he allowed him to take charge of the men who clearly respected him.

The field workers stepped aside for Abel, revealing a man lying on a blood-soaked bed. Abel expected a simple laborer, hurt from a hard day in the fields, and stared with surprise at the man fighting for his life.

Miguel Valencia, mid-30's with an expensive haircut and trimmed mustache, clutched his stomach with a bundle of bloody towels. He wore a tailored suit and tie, like Rodrigo and the other gentlemen he met when he first arrived, his gold jewelry and shined leather shoes a stark contrast with the crumbling bunkhouse and its residents. Miguel shook almost uncontrollably as he pressed the towels against his lower abdomen. Upon seeing Abel standing over him, he shut his eyes tight and spoke in bursts as he struggled to breathe in huge gasps.

"Fuck, Rigo," Miguel said, inhaling deeply and barking out his words. "You couldn't bring the doc?"

"Doctor is far... twenty mile... he already sleep."

"Then wake his ass up! That's what we pay him for!"

"Tell me," Abel said.

"Fall on pitchfork," Rigo said. "Unloading truck."

Abel found the explanation odd, but let it go. He grabbed Miguel's hand and looked him in the eye. "My name is Abel Grant."

Miguel glared at Abel as if he were insane. The field workers bowed their heads and prayed in Spanish.

"What's your name?" Abel asked.

"Rigo already told you..."

"You tell me."

"Miguel... Miguel Valencia."

With his free hand, Abel removed the towels from Miguel's stomach, revealing three small puncture wounds with steady streams of blood. He placed his free hand across them.

"Rigo!" Miguel said. "Call the doc! Get this fool off me!"

Abel quickly got the feeling. Miguel stopped shaking, the pain fading to a mild, throbbing bump in his gut. He grew calm, staring at the ceiling. After a moment, Abel released him and wiped the blood trickling from his mouth. "It's done."

Miguel lay unmoving on the sunken, bloody mattress. He looked about the room at all the work-worn faces staring at him. He slowly sat up, stubbornly refusing the help of the laborers as they watched him swing his legs over the edge of the bed. Amazed at his transformation, he ran his hand under his shirt to find the wound had disappeared.

"How you feel?" Rigo asked.

"I don't know. I feel like your legs, I guess. It's like the old man's wife said. I feel... light."

"How did this happen?" Abel asked, spitting a glob of blood into a towel.

"An accident. Fell off a truck and right onto a fuckin' pitchfork. Right in the gut. I should stay in the office where I belong."

"You were unloading a truck in an Armani suit?"

"A *ruined* Armani suit."

Miguel stood up and whipped off his jacket and shirt, his exposed torso covered in blood but fully healed. The field workers stood stunned. In hushed voices, they thanked God in Spanish, praising His name, praising the angel He sent to their simple bunkhouse in the vines.

Miguel handed his clothes to Abel.

"I'm not a tailor, Mr. Valencia. But I do require payment."

Miguel reached into his pants pocket and pulled out a roll of cash, no use of a wallet. Abel shook his head. "Something you made."

"I fuckin' made this," Miguel said, waving the thick roll of money in Abel's face.

"You earned that. I need something you made with your hands."

Miguel laughed at the odd demand and dropped the cash onto the bloody bed. He and Rigo walked through the dense crowd of onlookers and stepped outside. A moment later, they drove off in the blue utility vehicle.

Abel picked up the money, estimating it to be several thousand dollars. He noticed the many eyes upon him and held out the small fortune to them. They all backed away, scared of taking anything from God's Hand on Earth. Abel could feel their collective fear.

"Don't be afraid. It's mine to give, and now it's yours. Share it. Put it to good use. Respect my wishes."

One of the workers who knew English understood and felt the obligation to obey. He stepped forth and hesitantly took the money.

Abel walked to the open doorway and looked out across the vineyard to the mansion in the distance. He found the trail Rigo had used but ignored it, opting to follow a second trail through the vines, to the guest house a short trek to the west.

* * *

The next day, Abel sat alone at one of the many tables on the back patio of the manor, large enough to entertain a hundred guests. A cook worked a grill, nodding that food was coming shortly.

Rigo emerged from the house and joined Abel.

"Thank you again," Rigo said. "I never doubt... you are a living saint."

"English?"

"English.... always... at the house."

"You can speak Spanish with me, Rigo. I'm no tattle-tale. How's Mr. Valencia doing?"

Rigo felt relieved to speak his native language with his revered friend. "Like it never happened. I'll thank you again, for Miguel, and I apologize for him. He didn't show you respect."

"Accidents like this happen a lot?" Abel asked in Spanish.

"Every farm has its accidents. Workers get tired. They make mistakes."

"But Miguel's not exactly a worker, is he?"

Rigo changed the topic by waving to the cook and pointing to their empty wine glasses. The cook quickly uncorked a bottle. "David says that a guest should never hold an empty glass." The cook walked to their table and poured wine for them, bowing to Rigo as he returned to his grill.

"You've certainly come a long way," Abel said, swirling and sniffing his wine as he'd been taught.

"What do you mean?"

"When we first met, you were a worker like the men in the fields. But look at you now. It's what we call a meteoric rise."

"David sees talent. Loyalty."

"Must've done something big to catch his eye, to steal you from Brennan. He said you were loyal, too."

Rigo felt uneasy by the direction their conversation had taken. He looked around to see if anyone else could hear, satisfied that the cook stood just far enough away. "Thank you again, also, for what you did for me. I can never repay you."

"You thank me too many times, Rigo, and it will become undone."

Rigo looked alarmed until Abel grinned. The two men shared a laugh while the cook served them a platter of sausages and vegetables. Rigo nodded thanks and waited for him to leave. "What else did Brennan say about me?"

"He said he threatened to have you deported."

"And my mother and my sister. That's when I accepted David's offer." Rigo chose his next words carefully. "I know how to handle a hard day's work in the vines, and I don't get in the way of the field workers."

"I'm not talking about picking grapes or unloading trucks. I'm talking about getting shot." Rigo poorly feigned confusion. "Be honest with me, Rigo. I am a living saint, after all."

"He was stuck with a pitchfork. That's all. I mean, I didn't see it happen, but..."

Abel reached into his shirt pocket and placed three spent bullets on the table. "I pulled these out of him."

Rigo abandoned his flimsy cover story. Even as the sight of the bullets sent a shiver through him, he felt relieved that he suddenly had no choice but to come clean. Still, he would only drip feed the truth. "Miguel is trouble when he drinks."

"So he was shot because he was drinking? Not working. For David."

"I can tell you that Bellini is not one to be challenged. One of his men - Antonio - stood up to him at a company party, drunk, they say. No one's seen him since."

Rosemary stepped out of the house and spotted the two men across the patio. She approached them, prompting Rigo to quickly switch back to his limited English.

"Do you like... the wine?" Rigo asked, shifting the topic. "This is many people favorite."

"I'd love to know whose favorite that is because it's far from mine," Rosemary said, standing behind them.

"Don't be modest." Abel savored another sip.

"I'm being truthful. Put down that dishwater and come with me. You've clearly got a lot more to learn about wine."

* * *

Rosemary led Abel downstairs to an impressive wine cellar, a labyrinth of rooms that stored thousands of vintages, nearly as large as the guest house he spent the night in.

"Bellini Family Wines is not the first name that comes to mind with most oenophiles," Rosemary said as she perused the walls. "Truth be told, most of our wines are mixed into a stew or quaffed by hoboes. Here, you'll find the best, wines that elude the Rodrigos of the world." She passed a dozen racks before singling out a bottle for her guest. "1998 Chardonnay. Good year. Many awards. Consider it a gift to further your education."

"From David?"

"From me. David would give you a bottle of his masterpiece, La Donna Tempesta. But I promise, this Chard is no slouch."

"We shared La Donna when I first arrived. 'Masterpiece' is the word."

"The master himself would agree." She reached into another rack and handed him a second bottle. "This Donna is from a later year, but still worthy. Supposedly, he named it after me."

"So you're La Donna Tempesta, the 'Queen of the Storm'?"

"Very good. He says that I'm the peaceful calm in the center of the storm. I suppose it's because I'm the only person here who doesn't create fires for him to put out."

"Sounds like my wife, Regina."

"The angel is married?" Rosemary asked, curious.

"Widower. She's *my* queen."

"She was."

Abel nodded thanks and took his Chardonnay to the stairs.

"Wait. Stay a moment." Rosemary looked through the racks and chose another bottle for him. "When David learned about Miguel, he was speechless. That told me everything. He wants you to stay."

"I'm honored, but I've been here long enough. I'm needed in the city."

"Just for harvest week. A few more days. He says we're at a turning point for the company. Another '98."

"No more hoboes."

Rosemary laughed, feeling more relaxed with her guest. She took another two bottles and joined him on the stairs. "Getting you to come here was always my idea."

Abel wasn't sure to make of that last, odd comment, or her clarification that Regina was no longer his wife. He filed her comments and loaded offer in his mind, next to Rigo's fearful warning.

# 8

# A Good Time

Carlos parked his vintage Impala in front of the North Star Arms and pulled his toolbox from the trunk. As he walked up the stairs, he looked back at his precious lowrider surrounded by the tenements of H Street, all aglow from the approaching sunset. He saw it as an ugly yet striking picture of urban decay, bringing to mind an article from one of his car magazines. Photographers called that time of day "Golden Hour" because of the warm aura it cast upon everything, a brief window when all the world was beautiful, often ethereal. He couldn't help but take a photo of his ride, his phone camera's low resolution be damned.

He carried his tools into the building, went up to the third floor, and took a right turn, stopping at the last door of the hall. As Abel said, the door stood ajar, as it had for several weeks.

Carlos set his toolbox on the floor and knelt beside the doorknob. He quickly realized that the problem lay not only in the knob but in the worn door jamb, which had a crudely chamfered hole bored into the wood instead of a steel strike plate, another telltale sign of a slum lord. The supposedly simple repair would take longer than he figured.

From down the hall, next to the central stairs, Armen stepped out of his apartment. The old Russian quickly spotted the large gangster at his tenant's door, his tank top exposing his many tattoos.

"You fix or you break in?" Armen asked in his thick accent, locking the three properly installed deadbolts on his door, hardware paid out of pocket.

Carlos laughed at the curt old man and his insinuation. "Do I look like the kinda guy who'd break into a shithole like this?"

"Yes."

"Well, I don't break in, I fix. You must be the fuckin' slum lord I heard so much about."

"No, bro. Fucking slum lord live in fucking Hancock Park. He never come. I just collect rent, fix sink, fix toilet, fix other thing."

"Too bad you don't fix doors."

"I place work order for door," Armen said as he stepped onto the stairs. "You are him?"

"Sure, why not? I'm him."

"Very good. Six other unit after. Put invoice under door when you finish." Armen pointed to the bottom of his apartment door, nodded goodbye, and headed downstairs.

Carlos hadn't intended to spend his evening repairing the many busted doors of the North Star Arms - a bottle of white tequila awaited him back at the motel - but he knew his boss would appreciate the gesture, always encouraging him to help the community whenever the opportunity arose. With nothing else on his calendar, he begrudgingly set his mind to fixing all of his boss's neighbors' doors.

Six minutes later, Abel's old doorknob sat in Carlos's toolbox, replaced with the older yet perfectly functioning knob from the motel's former pizza parlor. Next came the door jamb. Looking over the half-finished job, he readied a metal strike plate, also taken from the shuttered pizza parlor, but realized it wouldn't be enough for the badly worn frame. He prepared some wood putty, but paused when he heard a loud crash and an argument coming from next door. It sounded like a man pleading with a woman, but Carlos could only make out bits and pieces.

*"Come on, girl... don't you... stir up shit tonight..."*
*"I ain't puttin' up with... I told you already..."*
*"Why you wanna... don't be like that..."*
*"I said last time... ain't messin' around..."*
*"Don't I pay you enough... maybe another girl..."*
*"I'm tired of this shit Felix..."*
*"Don't be a bitch... you're being too... just a good time..."*

The second-to-last apartment was further down the hall, yet the argument came through the thin walls as if the couple was standing over Carlos. He didn't recognize the man's voice, for he hadn't heard it before, but he recognized the name.

Felix.

Carlos heard the other door open and turned to his work, hiding his face behind the frame. The couple stepped into the hall, and from the corner of his eye, Carlos saw a young Mexican-American woman in a gaudy silk dress emerge with Brennan's bodyguard. As they went downstairs, Carlos wondered what the hell Felix was doing at Abel's building, and if the woman was in any trouble.

Knowing that the woman was likely Abel's friend, he felt obliged to send a text to his boss...

*"At your place now. Girl next door just left with Mr. Felix. Thought you should know."*

Carlos mixed the wood putty and smeared it on the door jamb when he received an unexpected response from his boss...

*"Follow."*

He'd only applied a dab of the putty when he read the dreaded message. He muttered a curse, put down his tools, and sent another text, hoping that would be the end of it.

*"Why? What am I supposed to do?"*

He waited a moment, hoping his boss would let the matter go, though he knew better.

*"Protect."*

Carlos threw down his putty knife. As much as he resented working as a handyman, he had no desire to watch over a prostitute and her John, especially one who stood ready to plug a bullet into his boss two days before. He sent another text.

"*She's a working girl. He's a client. She does this every night.*"

The former gang enforcer sat on the floor in the open doorway and awaited further instructions, again hoping Abel would dismiss it and allow him the evening once his repair work was done. His phone beeped, and he read Abel's response.

"*Follow. Protect Marci.*"

Carlos recognized her name from Abel's many stories about his neighbors. Of all the tenants at the North Star Arms, Marci Williams had the closest friendship with him. He'd long searched for a way to help her without burning their trust or revealing his identity, and he considered her safety paramount.

Carlos wiped his putty knife on a rag and shoved it back into his toolbox, regretting telling his boss about her unusual client. He sent one last text before heading downstairs.

"*I follow, Boss.*"

As Carlos carried his toolbox back to his car, catching Felix's sedan driving away, he got another text from his boss.

"*Be careful Big Man.*"

Driving his Impala well below the speed limit, Carlos repeated the words "follow protect" in his mind, spoken with Abel's voice, as he followed Mr. Felix's sedan several miles across the St. Nelia District to Warehouse Row. With the sun set behind the city, he knew the night and overcast sky helped keep him from view as he parked around a corner and watched Marci enter the storage complex with Brennan's man. Once they were inside, he stepped out of his car and approached the warehouse, peering through a broken, dirty window. He hoped for a garden variety stripper-for-hire gig, like a standard bachelor party, with a few men watching a woman dance half-naked to Classic Rock. Recalling the argument heard from the hallway, he had a feeling he was being overly optimistic.

He saw Mr. Felix leave Marci in a vast room of crates and dormant machinery and heard rap music play from a boom box somewhere with no signs of trouble. Just as he wondered what the point was of him tailing her there, he saw five other men enter with wide smiles, eager for their evening's entertainment. Marci danced to the thumping bass invitingly, seducing them with her moves. As she stripped for them, one man took a swig from a tall bottle, passing it to his associates. Their intense stares unnerved Carlos, for he knew how such men behaved with a paid woman behind closed doors, reminding him of his own sordid past.

"You're crazy, girl," Carlos said, muttering out in the cold as clouds gathered overhead. "But I get it. Money is money."

A light rain came down, soon drenching him, and he thought about abandoning his little mission and leaving Marci to her nightly work. His dismissal of the scene vanished when he saw a second man grab her by her hair and pull her down to the floor to the shouting cheers of his comrades. The sudden escalation reminded Carlos that he sat at that window unarmed yet tasked with protecting the young woman. He hoped that little act of aggression would be it, but again, he knew better.

He ran through the rain back to his lowrider and rummaged through the trunk for anything that could be used as a weapon. The closest thing he could find was a long flathead screwdriver. Though he wished for a gun or knife, both banned by his boss, he knew that simple tool would serve its purpose in his hands.

Returning to the window, Carlos peeked inside in time to see Marci grab a can of mace from her purse and spray a third man, making him scream in pain, eliciting mocking laughter from the rabid, drunk group like a circle of predators toying with their prey. He wanted her bold defense to be enough, wanted the belligerent men to get the message, but a fourth man rushed her, knocking the mace from her hands. Two other men grabbed her from behind, one of them receiving a vicious slash from Marci's nails, halting the laughter to an eerie silence.

Shit.

Carlos feared his building rage but no longer tethered it as he gripped the long screwdriver tight and entered through a nearby door, thrusting it open with a loud metallic boom. The five jackals looming over Marci turned toward him, instantly forgetting about her, for Carlos had suddenly become their entertainment. One of them recognized him and wisely backed away. Unfortunately for the rest of the group, their ignorance and bravado overcame them as they prepared for a brawl.

If only they had raised their hands in surrender and realized how poorly they mistreated Marci. If only they knew they were trapped in a warehouse with Carlos Cruz, a monster unleashed by their cruelty and further empowered by the divine protection of the living Saint Abel. Marci recognized the intimidating gangster and ran behind him, gathering her things. She stood and watched as he advanced toward the rowdy pack, the simple screwdriver held like a weapon.

Never in her wildest imagination could she have foreseen the brutality of her ward as he grabbed the men and impaled their thighs with the long tool, slashing at their faces and breaking their arms backward. He stomped their heads to the concrete floor and pummeled them to a pulp against the corrugated steel walls. Marci watched the scene with shock and curiosity. Carlos could have easily killed those men, but maimed them instead. She'd secretly suspected Abel of being "The Angel of St. Nelia" but also surmised Carlos as his appointed servant. It would certainly explain why the feared criminal left his brethren to inexplicably follow Abel throughout the day, though the gruesome scene cast doubt. Seeing how easily he dispatched her aggressors, how violent he became on her behalf, she realized there could have been twenty men in that room, and they'd have all be doomed to fall to his mission. Though he guarded Abel, and now fought for her protection, she wondered if such a frightening beast could truly be a servant of God.

Minutes later, Carlos stood surrounded by the bloody bodies of the men who dared to accost one of his boss's confidants. It had been years since he confronted a mob in such a bloody melee, but each strike felt alarmingly natural to him, each wound shared as Reverend Dean had always preached. Though it pained him to send them all to the floor, alive but clinging to life, he knew Abel would have him do whatever it took to protect Marci.

"Jesus, did you have to fuck them up so bad?" Marci asked.

"These guys?" Carlos asked. "Yeah, I had to."

As Carlos escorted Marci outside, he saw Mr. Felix approach from across the property. He gestured for Marci to get in the car as he waited for Felix to continue the scene. The two men stood just ten paces apart, locking eyes through the dense rain. Felix turned to peer into the warehouse at his men flailing on the floor.

"You did this?" Mr. Felix asked, shouting over the rain.

"No, 'Mr. Felix.' Your boys did this."

"A bit extreme."

"We both know asking pretty please wouldn't have worked." He held the long screwdriver high, ensuring Felix a good look at the blood dripping from its flathead tip. "You next?"

Mr. Felix was no fool. Though he had a pistol in his coat pocket, he kept his hands at his side. He knew that even if he plugged a bullet into Carlos, the man would still rush him like a bear and jam the screwdriver deep into his neck seconds after. He could already feel it wedged in his throat. Hiding his apprehension, he remained fixed on Carlos. "You realize I gotta tell the old man about all this."

"Tell him it was Carlos Cruz. C-R-U-Z. Tell him you know where to find me, and that I'll be waiting."

"You won't be waiting long."

"Good," Carlos said defiantly. "I fuckin' hate waiting."

"This really what you want? For a whore? For that arrogant asshole you follow?"

"Come for me in the middle of the night when I'm asleep." Carlos walked to his car. "I'll leave the door unlocked."

Carlos sat behind the wheel of his Impala and started the engine. He drove out of the lot, but stopped at the street, looking back at Mr. Felix in the rain through his rearview mirror. He shifted into Reverse, pulled up beside Felix and rolled his window down for a final warning. "And if my arrogant asshole boss even crosses your mind, I'm coming back with more than a fuckin' screwdriver."

The two men stared at each other. Felix again gripped the pistol in his coat but hesitated to use it, even though Carlos now sat seemingly defenseless in his car. If Abel Grant was indeed an angel, Carlos Cruz was surely his personal devil.

Carlos rolled up his window and drove Marci home. She clung to her can of mace even as she sat beside her guard. Sixteen silent minutes later, they pulled over in front of the North Star Arms. Carlos shifted into Park and waited for her to get out.

"I coulda taken care of myself," Marci said.

"I'm sure you could've."

"This ain't the first time, you know."

"After tonight, it's the last."

"What's gonna happen to me if they come back?"

"They won't."

"But what if they do?" she asked, afraid to return to her apartment alone.

"Then I'll kill them all."

Marci felt a chill at Carlos's calm demeanor after having brutalized five men and threatening a mob enforcer. "Abel... he's the angel, ain't he? He sent you, right?"

"Go home," Carlos said, nodding for her to get out.

"I mean, why else would you give a shit about me gettin' roughed up?"

"Go home. Don't tell no one about this."

"Or what?"

Carlos understood her hesitation. He thought about his boss and what he might say. "Or else everything gets undone."

Marci stepped out of the lowrider and turned for a final word. "Thanks."

"Thank *him*. I was just supposed to fix a door."

Marci headed up the stairs to her apartment while Carlos drove away, back to his bottle of white tequila, awaiting him at the Royal Queen Motel.

# 9

# Every Man's Misfortune

Another line of homeless people stretched around the parking lot of St. Nelia Church, waiting for boxes of donated food and sundries, while a large group gathered at the rear of a newly arrived truck for secondhand clothes. Reverend Dean walked out of the church and joined his volunteers at the head of the food line. He picked up a box, but Arlo promptly took it from him and pulled him aside for a private word. To the reverend's dismay, his trustee led him to a Dodge Viper parked behind the truck, out of view.

"Where is he?" the reverend asked.

"Your office, last I checked."

"Did anyone else see him?"

"I dunno. Maybe not. Everybody's busy."

"Stay out here, Arlo. Keep calm. Business as usual."

"I'm comin' in with you."

"No, I'll be okay. I need you out here."

Reverend Dean smiled at his flock as he returned to the church, went down the left hall and into his office, where he saw Brennan sitting at his desk, using his computer. He saw Mr. Felix at the old coffee machine, trying to figure out how to work it.

"Good morning, Michael." Reverend Dean spoke in a carefully polite tone, as if any odd inflection or poor choice of words might trigger a bomb.

"It's strange hearing my name. Everyone calls me 'Brennan.' Only the Honorable Reverend Dean McCall has the stones to call me 'Michael.'"

"Your mother named you Michael, I call you Michael. Should I not?"

"I hated my mother, you should know." Brennan continued to browse the reverend's computer. "But I kinda like the formality of it, to be honest. It's refreshing. How's the Sunday School doing?"

"Wonderful. You did God's good work."

"I figure there should be a ceremony to christen it the 'Michael Nicholas Brennan Education Center.' Has a nice ring, don't it? I mean, my ex don't go here no more, but the building still stands. My money's still spent."

Reverend Dean turned to Mr. Felix, still struggling with the coffee maker. "Let me get that. Two coffees?"

"From that relic? Why not? A little Wild Turkey will help it go down."

The reverend dumped out the old coffee, rinsed the carafe, and prepared a new pot. "I apologize. I would've had fresh coffee ready, but I didn't see you come in."

"They told me you were in the can. It sounded kinda funny. You never think about it, but men of the cloth are just like any other mortal man. They gotta take a mean shit from time to time. Gotta exorcize the evil waste."

"That's an odd way to put it." Reverend Dean forced a laugh.

Brennan leaned back in his chair. He cut and lit a cigar and took a puff, blowing smoke across the small office. "Makes sense to me. I've always been told that your body is a temple, like this church. Shit packing your intestines is like the city's riffraff crowding these sacred halls. Can't have crackheads and whores pitching camp in the chapel, now can you? That's why there comes a time every evening where you gotta shove that shit out the door."

Reverend Dean didn't like the man's analogy or his presence, but continued trying to placate him. "How can I help you, Michael?"

"You still pray for me, Reverend?"

"Every day. I pray for many."

"Thanks, but you can unsubscribe me from that list. I can testify, prayin' don't do jack shit. The Lord don't listen, least not when it comes to me."

Reverend Dean set two mugs of coffee on the desk. Brennan pulled a flask from his coat pocket and poured whiskey into them both before he and his associate took sips.

"Much obliged," Brennan said. "Burnt black coffee and bourbon go good with a Maduro."

"Speaking of which, would you mind please putting that out?"

"In my condition, a cigar don't mean much, but thanks for your concern." Brennan puffed his cigar and gestured for the reverend to take the guest seat in front of his own desk. "Time for business. You know why I'm here, and it ain't for no box of expired beans and rice."

"I'm not sure what you mean." Reverend Dean sat down as told. He felt Mr. Felix looming behind him near the door.

"And I am sure you know exactly what I mean, or rather who I mean. Abel Grant. I already been to see him, so it's pointless to pretend."

"Why come to me? You already found him on your own."

"Yeah, but he didn't do shit for me. He pulled a bullet out of my gut, and I'm grateful, but my body still looks and feels like rotted meat. He didn't cure me, Reverend."

"Again, why come to me?"

"Convince him," Brennan said firmly.

Reverend Dean cleared his throat and regretted not making a cup of coffee for himself. It would have given his shaking hands something to do. "I can't convince him any more than I could convince your doctor. If he didn't heal you, it means he can't."

"That's where we see things differently. Hearing men say they can't do something, and then getting them to make it fuckin' happen, that's what I do. I have yet to take no from nobody."

Realizing that Abel would forever be in peril with Brennan always pursuing him, the reverend put his friend's mission ahead of his own trepidation. He swallowed his fear and affirmed himself, rising out of his chair to make his point. "Some things can't be bought, can't be forced. I know that's hard for a man like you to understand. He's not motivated by money and he can't undo every man's misfortune. I'm sorry, Michael."

Brennan took another puff of his cigar. He held in the smoke for a moment, as if considering the reverend's words, before exhaling it in disappointment. "You know, you really should lock your computer whenever you're not in here." He swiveled the computer monitor around to reveal a bank statement on the screen. The sight of the spreadsheet's figures silenced the reverend. "Quite a lot of lettuce is ready to transfer to your church. The angel was recently 'transferred' to Della Luna. Reverend, you know I don't like coincidences."

"What are you getting at, Michael..."

Mr. Felix grabbed Reverend Dean by his shoulders and slammed him back into his seat.

"David Bellini bought the angel. Please don't deny it. My men have been watching him for a while now. I know where he goes, who he talks to, how he takes *his* cup of coffee."

Reverend Dean remained silent. Brennan slugged his coffee and stood from the desk. "If I was you I'd keep an eye on that transfer. It's still pending, which means, unlike my cash donation, it's just a blinking dot on your computer. Your sudden fortune could just as suddenly become your misfortune."

Brennan and Mr. Felix walked out of the office. Reverend Dean sat frozen, waiting to hear the Dodge Viper's engine roar to life and drive away. He stood and shut the door, torn, unsure, before sitting at his desk to scrutinize the grayed out numbers on his computer.

*Transfer Pending.*

Outside the church, Arlo watched the sports car drive down the road. He excused himself from the food line and made a call on his cell phone.

"Brennan just left," Arlo said, ensuring that no one heard him.

"Of course," David Bellini said on the other end. "So now we know. You can expect payment within the week."

"Payment can be six months late for all I care. I just want that con artist away from the reverend. I dug up some background on him."

"Go on."

Arlo hesitated to reveal his discovery, but the sight of his beloved reverend emerging from the church visibly shaken empowered him. "Before he hooked up with Reverend Dean, he made a killing working a revival circuit in Texas. Look up Pastor Goldie Reeves."

# 10

# Child of God

The Kade Bowers Complex in Fort Worth, Texas was one of the largest convention centers in the nation when it first opened its doors in early 2012. It boasted 75 meeting rooms, an impressive 1,600-seat theater, and a staggering 9,500-seat arena. The sparkling new center had only been open for six months before Galen Riverdam, Jr. - known by the country's most devout as Pastor Goldie Reeves - held two Christian revivals there. Gathered together from all parts of Texas and the surrounding six southern states, his congregation fit inside the center's theater during its opening week, but ticket sales near 4,000 warranted use of the arena for his second visit.

Most of the expanded audience arrived in buses and caravans, many entering in wheelchairs and walkers, and though the crowd occupied less than half of the arena's capacity, their constant excitement and outbursts of joy made it feel like a packed house. They cheered for the jubilant evangelist as he ran back and forth across the stage like a showman, the 64-year-old man decked out in a white suit and dripping with gold jewelry. They loved his energy, his compassion, his over-the-top Cajun accent, and his little habits of running his hand across his thinning hair whenever he proclaimed "Amen!"

"I lookee out here and I see the sick'uns," Pastor Goldie said in a sudden hushed tone, silencing his flock. "I see here the weak, the sufferin', and though y'alls bodies may be kindling on the embers, I can feel your spirits is strong like oak. And I say AMEN!"

The crowd shouted "AMEN!" in response, their eyes widening and collective pulse rising as five men in designer suits took the stage, standing in a semi-circle behind the beloved pastor. The thousands of emotional men and women in the audience knew those men as Pastor Goldie Reeves's personal "angels," including their newest addition, Abel Grant, known on the revival circuit as "Brother Rapha." Since shuttering the blues club and selling his house two months before, he and Carlos joined the pastor's tour and lived in the finest hotels Texas offered, if only for a weekend at a time.

"But y'all didn't come to hear old Pastor Reeves blabber on. Behind me are five of God's genuine, bonafide, certified angels on Earth. I say AYY-MEN!"

The crowd cheered "AMEN!" back at the stage, cueing Abel to step forth and join Pastor Goldie who promptly threw his arm around his newest acolyte, sticking to their script with precision. Carlos stood in the wings with the other bodyguards and always winced whenever anyone, including the pastor, touched his boss.

"I got all my angels with me today! I got Brothers Abner, Elijah, Jonah, Gabriel, and right here with me we got us Brother Rapha! Delivered to the great City of Fort Worth as promised!"

The audience knew Brother Rapha well after his six past appearances resulted in miracles that even the most cynical critic had a tough time debunking. The four other angels were expert mentalists, illusionists, and brilliant all-around performers, and they certainly garnered the flock's attention, but there was something about Abel's Brother Rapha that felt refreshing and real. He made no gestures for praise, no fanciful dances, no calls for God's grace, and seemed uninterested in soaking up the adulation of the mesmerized masses before him.

"But let us not wait no further! I wanna see ol' Butchie Franklin up here, front and center, ready to receive The Lord! Where you at, Butchie?"

Along the west aisle, at the end of the fifth row, Butchie Franklin raised his hand from his wheelchair. The middle-aged African-American man wore army fatigues and boots. His face beamed as he wheeled himself to the front row where Brothers Elijah and Jonah took over, pushing the large man up a ramp and onto the stage.

Pastor Goldie seemed entranced by the army veteran as he approached, parking his wheelchair between him and Abel.

"Look at this mighty man! This hero! Served his country! Got his legs shot up fightin' for your freedom! How you feelin', Private Franklin?"

"I'm just happy to be here," Butchie said, barely able to contain himself.

"You should be, son, you definitely should be, 'cause Brother Rapha is gonna fix you up good!"

Abel knelt beside Butchie's wheelchair and placed his hands on his legs, paralyzed since his nearly fatal injury in Afghanistan a year before. An improvised explosive device detonated under his truck, costing his unit two lives and the use of his legs.

"Here it comes, y'all!" Pastor Goldie said to the crowd. "I can feel it comin'!"

As Abel got the feeling, gripping the soldier's legs tight, Pastor Goldie's floor staff passed around collection plates as they did whenever a member of the flock was being healed. With Brother Rapha as their newest draw, the donations flowed generously. By the time Butchie Franklin stood from his wheelchair for the first time in ten months, weeping in disbelief, the plates were overflowing.

* * *

Most evangelical revivals last between two and four hours, and are held for several days, but to give his events the "feel of Broadway," Pastor Goldie Reeves and his angels took the stage for six hours with an intermission. The grand, lengthy production and limited engagement allowed the pastor to bump up the ticket price from $50 to $75, bringing in around $300,000 before anyone set foot in the convention center. The sales of merchandise before and after the event, and during intermission, added another $60,000 to the cause.

At intermission, the pastor's staff counted and sorted the staggering additional cash donations from the many rounds of collection plates, the bills spilling over the sides of the four plastic folding tables set up backstage. Pastor Goldie likened the impressive payday to thirty years of Sunday services all in one afternoon.

Abel sat alone and exhausted on a couch in front of the tables. He nursed a can of soda as he stared at the seemingly endless stream of money. Pastor Goldie joined him, falling onto the couch with his arms outstretched.

"How we feelin'?" Pastor Goldie asked.

"I could use a smoke."

"You look like you could use a blood transfusion! Never seen a Black man lose color in his face before. You sure you okay, son?"

"I'll be ready for the next half, if that's what you're asking, Goldie." Abel rubbed the crucifix on his necklace.

"Fair enough. Hey, we done a lot of good here today."

"How much good?"

"Almost 400 Large so far, and it's not even lunch. Second crowd's already shuffling in. They been waiting in the rain for five hours! You're bigger than Elvis, my friend." Abel smiled at the ridiculous comparison. "And soon to be richer, too. You put on one hell of a show, son."

Carlos stood nearby, watching the ongoing cash count. He noticed Abel struggle to sit up on the couch and knew he'd been pushing himself hard all morning.

"Maybe he can take a break?" Carlos said. "This shit knocks the wind outta him, you know?"

"Ain't that what we're doing right now? Takin' a break? You sure a can of pop is enough? We got us a full bar back here."

"I mean, the next crowd. Tell 'em Abel's done for the day. We can always come back 'cause you know they will."

"Come back?" Pastor Goldie said with a laugh. "We're right here, right now, son."

"Boss comes back, we sell more tickets, make more money, if that's what's buggin' you."

Pastor Goldie reached for a nearby table and picked up a stack of cash. "Money certainly ain't buggin' me today. And I say we make hay while the sun is shinin'!"

"I'm okay, Big Man," Abel said, rubbing his crucifix again. He took slow, deep breaths, willing himself to recover quickly.

"If you say so, Boss. I follow you."

Pastor Goldie laughed and tossed the cash back onto the table. "Boys, ain't no cameras back here. As cute as it is, y'all can drop the messiah-disciple bit. Have a drink. Some powerful donors even sent cases of wine. The good stuff."

"Fuckin' hate wine," Carlos said. "Even the 'good stuff.'"

"Suit yourself." The pastor picked up a bottle of champagne from a case beside the couch. "I tell you boys, that soldier was priceless! When he started dancing around? Holy hell, that was something to behold. We need to bring him back for an encore."

Abel gave Pastor Goldie an incredulous look. "That isn't how it works..."

"Now, don't get nervous, but I gotta tell you before I forget. Ron Ellison is here. You know who Ron Ellison is, right?"

"The tech genius?"

"Well, I don't know about all that, but he's the third richest man in Texas, that's what I know. Got a sick boy, used to be a star quarterback. Bone cancer or something."

"Fine, bring him to the stage."

"No, Ellison gets a private session. Saturday. The man's lookin' to drop five figures, wants you as his personal savior."

Carlos felt uncomfortable with the pastor's proposal. He shot a look to his boss, who nodded to keep calm.

When Abel first approached Pastor Goldie at one of his revivals in Houston, he sought to exploit his gift out of anger toward God for what transpired that fateful night in the woods, something that always left a pit in his friend's stomach. As he healed the pastor's flock, and the events grew more grandiose, a pit grew within him as well. He felt fulfilled with the renewed life he offered people and no longer thought of the riches piling up around him. He started to see Pastor Goldie Reeves's roadshow for what it was, a thinly veiled fleecing of the masses, using their faith against them like a giant placebo.

"Also, we have Angel Ventana," Pastor Goldie said. "You know him, I'm sure. He wants his own private visit on Sunday."

"Angel Ventana?" Carlos said, alarmed. "The kingpin of coke? The fucker's a murderous psycho!"

"I get it, but I didn't cold call the bastard. He reached out to us! He's got a girl hooked up to a ventilator 24-7. The man has money and power. Men like that get what they want, and he wants Abel."

"Boss don't belong to no one."

"Carlos, son, don't think if it as 'belong.' It's more like a rental kinda thing, like if you hired a clown to entertain a birthday party."

"Is that what I am?" Abel asked, affronted by the analogy, overwhelmed by the sudden news.

"You know what I mean," Pastor Goldie said. "Don't get all touchy-feely on me now." The pastor checked the time on his gold watch and stood from the couch. "Looks like you're up, Brother Rapha."

The audience grew by another thousand, taking their seats as Pastor Goldie and his angels returned to the stage. Abel looked out at the new faces and readied himself for another line of sick and suffering.

Four men approached the stage down the center aisle, led by Angel Ventana, a 40-year-old giant in a black suit that matched his slicked back hair. He held his sleeping pre-teen daughter, Jenny, and lifted her petite frame above his head, placing her upon the stage. He and his entourage backed away, standing side-by-side in the front row.

Pastor Goldie and Abel stood dumbstruck, their careful script thrown to the wind by the unexpected visitor.

"Mr. Angel Ventana is here!" Pastor Goldie said to the crowd, swerving to improvise. "An honor! Didn't see you on the list! We were set on seeing young Jenny on Sunday morning."

"Every day is Sunday in the eyes of God," Ventana said. "Ain't that right, Pastor?"

"We do think alike, sir, yes we do. Great minds, you know." Pastor Goldie turned to Abel, his eyes barely hiding sudden panic. "Brother Rapha! Won't you chase the devil out of sleepyhead little Jenny? Let her wake up a new girl!"

Abel knelt her and placed his hands on her arms. He moved his grip a few times - across her heart, over her forehead, on her stomach - but felt nothing. His look of confusion prompted unsure chatter from the audience.

"The Lord's work is different with each Child of God y'all! " Pastor Goldie said, pacing the stage. "Brother Rapha just needs a moment!"

Still on his knees, Abel continued to search the girl for her sickness within, waiting for the feeling to come. He glanced at Angel Ventana and his men down in the front row, at Pastor Goldie standing above him, and at Carlos waiting in the wings, as he realized something was terribly wrong.

"I'm sorry," Abel said, releasing the girl. "I can't help her." He remained on his knees and stared at her peaceful face.

The crowd murmured concern, hundreds of whispers building to a wave of thousands that ranged from curiosity to frustration to dread. Ventana heard the many onlookers wondering aloud. Unaccustomed to being denied, he and his men climbed onto the stage and loomed over Abel and Jenny.

"Help her," Ventana said. "She's traveled a long way. God told me to bring her here today, to put her in your hands."

"Brother Rapha just needs time!" Pastor Goldie said, his showman voice assuring everyone from the arena's speakers. "And space! Everyone please back up!" The pastor had never seen Abel fail to "heal" someone. Believing him to be a crowd-entrancing con man like his others, one more talented than any he'd ever seen in all his years on the grift, he couldn't fathom why Abel now refused to perform.

"I said I can't help her," Abel said firmly.

Pastor Goldie knelt down beside Abel as if to pray. He bowed his head and pressed his face against his shoulder to hide his whispering. "What the hell is wrong with you? Wake her up! Coax her to stand at least! You know who this man is?"

"You have the wrong idea about me, Goldie."

"God came to me in a dream," Ventana said. "He told me to come here today. We made the long drive from Arizona because you're supposed to help us, Brother Rapha..."

"My name is Abel Grant." Having damn enough of the charade, he stood and offered his hand to Ventana. "Your daughter is beyond my help. I'm sorry."

The crowd grew restless, with shouts of both support and protest. Those familiar with Abel's past appearances gave him the benefit of the doubt, thinking his divine gift surely can't help everyone. Those new to the revival scene fell back to their cynical uncertainty. Pastor Goldie looked out at his audience, who started following him soon after witnessing his many miracles, and knew he was just as quickly losing them.

"I told you, son," Pastor Goldie whispered in his mock prayer, "the Who's Who of Texas is sittin' in the front row. And this man will shoot up this entire place if you don't perform NOW."

Ventana's confusion merged with anger. He looked back at his men before turning back to Abel. "You want more money? Is that it?"

To the pastor's dismay, the stage mics picked up every word of the tense exchange.

"Keep your money," Abel said.

"I can give you whatever you want! Name it!"

"All your riches can't help you." Abel looked at Jenny.

"Then what the hell do you want?"

"I want to know when this girl died."

Pastor Goldie stood and turned to the shocked audience, seeing many shuffling into the aisle and leaving the arena. "We're gonna take a little break, see if we can work this out. We just need to take the time to..."

"'This girl' is my daughter!" Ventana said, his voice bellowing across the stage, his hands clinched into fists.

Abel stood and glared at the crime boss, unmoved by his show of dominance. "You drove across three states with your dead child?"

Angel Ventana, the feared drug lord whose empire stretched from California to New Mexico, dropped his machismo and cried, his sudden sorrow flashing to a fury. He gestured for his men to take Jenny's body away as he rushed Abel, grabbing him by the throat, prompting Carlos to run onto the stage to intervene.

"This girl is my daughter!" Ventana screamed. "A child of God! Why do you deny me His power? What game are you fuckin' playing?"

Ventana clocked Abel with a sucker punch, knocking him down into the front row below. Carlos tackled him and landed several powerful blows before pinning him to the stage. A brawl broke out between Ventana's men and the pastor's staff, sending the audience scrambling for the exits. During the brutal melee, Pastor Goldie ran off stage.

Ventana struck Carlos in the jaw and rose to his feet. As Carlos was jumped by two of his men, Ventana yelled out at the panicked crowd and at Abel on the floor below. "You son of a bitch! Where is God? Where is He when I need Him?"

Sprawled out in the front row, Abel looked up at the pandemonium, at Carlos struggling in the chaos, at Pastor Goldie running out a side door, and the dead girl now to the side of the stage. He ripped off his crucifix necklace and tossed it at Ventana's feet. The drug lord fumed as he jumped off the stage and yelled inches from Abel's face.

"Where is He? I DEMAND TO KNOW! Where is He?"

"He's up there!" Abel said, seething with rage. "Laughing at our pain! This gift is not for you! Just as it wasn't for me!"

Ventana pulled out a gun and pointed it at Abel, but saw in his face that 'the angel' he sought to control wasn't afraid to die. Abel looked down the gun barrel and stared at the criminal, almost daring him to pull the trigger.

A defeated Ventana pocketed his gun and stomped him in the face.

# 11

# A Cruel World

The guest house at Bellini Family Wines sat well behind the mansion, surrounded by 130 acres of hillside vines and nestled within a small grove of ancient oak. Two paths led to the front door: a 25-minute walk south to the main house and a 10-minute walk northwest to the field workers' bunkhouse further into the property. With a large bedroom, bathroom, living room, kitchen, and a full-length porch, the guest house was a luxury cottage home, and though the family had it built 89 years after the mansion, it shared its elder's Colonial charm of red brick and white trim.

Abel sat at the small dining table of his temporary home. Staring at a large wooden crucifix mounted high on the living room's accent wall. Below it, near Jesus Christ's feet, was an antique cabinet housing a bookshelf stereo with a dual-cassette deck, an innovative feature from Abel's youth. He switched on the stereo's radio, but only a handful of A.M. stations were picked up in those rolling hills, none of which suited him. Expecting to stumble upon a few cassettes, he opened the cabinet and was surprised to find ten shoeboxes filled with a mint-condition selection sorted by genre. Whoever arranged that lovely little house had an eclectic taste in music.

After thumbing through decades of doo-wap, dance club hits, hard rock, and new wave, he found a cassette labeled "Legendary Blues Classics Vol. 1." He opened the case to find it empty, and opted for a Mozart compilation instead. When he opened the deck door, he discovered that the blues cassette was already in place. Curious, he pressed Play and heard a familiar tune - Bessie Smith's "Baby Won't You Please Come Home."

Livia.

The young girl had been charged with preparing the guest house for him. In the event that Abel chose to stay at the estate through harvest week, she'd taken the liberty of cueing the blues cassette to that special song she heard in his apartment.

As the song's intro played, and Bessie's voice came out of the twin speakers on the sides of the cabinet, the benevolent specter of his late wife appeared. Regina sat in his seat at the dining room table, her white gown flapping from a breeze coming from the open patio door. As always, Abel could not see her, but could feel her near as if she had always been there, waiting for him to summon her.

"Nice place," Regina said.

"I suppose so, but I still don't know why I'm here."

"You saved two people, baby. That's no small thing."

Abel looked up at the tall wooden crucifix. "But I'm not sure I should have. Can you ever truly save someone? Even Jesus died, a corpse to rot in the sun."

"He came back, so they say."

"He did come back, that much I know." Abel shut the cabinet and sat in an armchair in the center of the living room. "He came back to a cruel world that only got worse. The Romans were still in power. People still suffered. Centuries of war and inquisitions in His name. Seeing all that, I wonder if His sacrifice meant anything to Him. I wonder if it shook His own faith."

"It sure shook yours."

Regina walked behind Abel's chair and hugged his neck and shoulder from behind. "Forgive them, for they know not what they do."

"Am I to lose myself as I save them?"

"Saviors serve others as they suffer unto themselves. You know that." She walked around the armchair and stood in front of Abel.

Abel considered her words, something he'd told himself many times over many nights freezing at the old motel or on the worn mattress of his tenement apartment. He faintly saw her bright silhouette aligned with the crucifix behind her, a rare sight that only happened when his heart ached in her presence. He wished to gaze upon her face, but felt grateful to see her at all.

"Damn this gift," Abel said in a hushed exhale, as if to keep Regina from hearing him. "The price He made me pay..."

* * *

A winding two-lane road cut through the Devil's Backbone, a scenic 51-mile drive of rolling limestone hills, sweeping valleys, and miles of shoreline around Canyon Lake. During the day, the loop drive offered breathtaking views of the Edwards Plateau of Texas. At night, it proved an intimidating route, not only for its many blind corners and sudden hairpins but also for the rumors of ghosts that plagued the byway - Spanish monks, Native Americans, Confederate soldiers, and lost travelers.

Regina Grant had enough difficulty driving Abel's Corvette, never having mastered a stick shift, but her frustration was compounded when she turned off I-35 a full half-hour too soon while her tipsy husband dozed in the passenger seat.

She and Abel had been heading south to San Antonio, to her agent's birthday party, where she was to sing a classic blues song for him and a room full of his peers in the music industry. She cursed at herself for being late to such an important event, not realizing that her expectant audience - nor anyone else - would never hear her sing again.

With only her headlamps to light the way, the twisty road stretched into the woods surrounding Canyon Lake, into the heart of the Devil's Backbone. Like other native Texans, she grew up hearing stories of the vengeful ghosts that roamed the desolate wooded area, but never heeded them until she desperately tried to navigate their domain.

Failing to calm herself, her tires skidded upon each tight turn, skirting the sandy shoulders that bordered a drop to the massive Ash and Live Oak trees below.

"Baby Won't You Please Come Home" played on a loop on the stereo to familiarize Regina with the lyrics in preparation for her performance. She sang along with Bessie Smith, trying to distract herself from her growing anxiety. Every few minutes, she'd nudge Abel, but he was nearly out cold from too many pre-party highballs of cognac, muttering "You got this, Regina" and "Just slow down is all," worthless advice when ghosts chased you through the dark hills in the middle of the night.

The last thing Regina saw was a pair of high beams racing toward her around a narrow hairpin, forcing her to swerve and stomp the brakes, all while fumbling with the damn stick. The nightmare began with a series of strange sensations, all striking her at once.

The piercing sound of the squealing tires...
The unnerving feeling of the car flying off the cliff road...
The crash of shattered glass and crumpled metal...
The sudden impact and deafening silence.

Abel had been dreaming of the opening night of his club. With a full house enjoying martinis and the musical styling of a local jazz band, he and Regina stood in wait behind the bar, dressed in their finest formal wear. Abel had donned a tuxedo while Regina chose a black dress whose sequins sparkled under the bar's overhead lamps. As the audience applauded the jazz trio's finale, the Grants joined them on stage. Abel sat behind his piano while his elegant wife stood at the microphone stand, her slender shape silhouetted by the stage lights at her feet. As Abel curled his fingers over the keys, he realized he forgot their opening song. His wife sang without his accompaniment, her voice echoing as if she stood in a great hall, and the still audience slipped away into the dark. Abel mashed his hands on the keys, trying to recall their chosen grand opening tune, creating a frightening crash that only he could hear. To his fright, he hadn't merely forgotten the tune. He forgot how to play.

He again looked up at his wife, but like her devout audience, she, too, had slipped into the darkness, as did the jazz trio, the piano, and the rest of the club.

He sat alone on stage, surrounded by a black void, his hands cold as ice, his mind lost in panic, somehow knowing that it was all gone forever.

Abel awoke atop dead leaves on torn branches, sprawled out in a clearing in the woods. His head felt thick and heavy, his tuxedo was drenched in mud, and his hands and arms were streaked with blood and embedded with rocks and twigs. He pushed himself off the ground but quickly fell over with a sharp pain, his right hand and arm a lacerated mess. The silence of the Devil's Backbone and the ominous sight of the Live Oaks that towered over him sent chills through his body, overwhelming him as he tried to piece together where he was and what had ripped him from his idyllic dream.

Struggling to stand, he saw a flashing red light across the mud. He turned to find its source, but there was nothing around as far as he could see. A soft whine of settling metal caught his ear, and he looked up to see his Corvette entangled high in a massive oak tree. Above that was the cliff road they'd been driving on. All at once, he realized Regina had driven off the road and plunged the car into the tree. The impact threw him out and onto the dead leaves and shallow mud of the ground below.

He peered up at the wreck and saw his wife in the twisted mangle of metal, trapped in the tree.

"Regina!" He screamed her name again without waiting for a reply. "Regina!"

His right arm throbbing in pain, he stumbled to the base of the tree and looked up at the car's undercarriage directly above him. The faint sound of Bessie Smith's "Baby Won't You Please Come Home" continued on the car stereo in an endless loop, a cruel soundtrack contrasting with their plight.

"Regina! You hold on! I'm coming!"

With one good arm and legs soaked from the freezing mud bog, he strained to pull himself up the tree, each branch an agonizing effort. Nearly ten minutes later, he sat beside his wrecked car, 30 feet off the ground, with a full view of his wife. Her white evening gown was splattered with blood, shattered glass clinging to her hair. The dashboard crumpled from the crash and pinned her to the bent steering wheel. With the passenger seat between them, and his right arm hanging worthless, he couldn't reach her.

"Regina baby, say something! You with me! Regina!"

She remained unmoving, her eyes shut, her head tilted to the side. For a moment, Abel held his breath and feared the worst, while Bessie Smith crooned as if for the last time. He rubbed his crucifix with such fervor that it started to feel hot.

She finally opened her eyes.

"Abel..."

"Regina! Thank God! You hold on!"

"I should... learn to drive stick."

Abel laughed until he couldn't breathe, his breathy gasps turning to cries. "I'll teach you when we get back home. With this arm banged up, you're gonna be driving us around for a while."

"Get... an automatic."

He laughed again, coughing up blood, as he forced his upper body into the car, the busted window carving into his ribs. He reached out for her hand, only inches away, but couldn't make contact. Abel took a moment to catch his breath, only to be jolted to terror as Regina shut her eyes again.

"Regina! REGINA!"

# 12

# Now We Shake Hands

Livia got in the farm utility vehicle behind the manor, ready to drive her father into the vineyard underneath another overcast morning sky. She started the engine, but shut it off when she saw Abel approaching after his long walk from the guest house.

"Good morning, sunshine," she said. "Slept well?"

"Slept very well. The accommodations were perfect. Sadly, I didn't wake up well."

"Pillows not soft enough?"

"Had a bad dream."

"S'yeah, you did put away a lot of Merlot last night, so you only got yourself to blame. Can't you wave your hand and heal a raging hangover?"

"Can't heal myself, unfortunately."

David walked up to them and sat in the utility vehicle, intrigued by Abel's words.

"Some angel you are," Livia said. "What good are super powers if you still wake up with wino headaches?" She glanced at her father, then back at Abel. "Hey, you wanna come with? Pop's cranking up a new bottling station. Come on, hop in the mule."

"Mule?"

"Mom called this thing 'The Blue Mule,'" she said, banging a fist onto the tubular steel door of the utility vehicle. "Since then, everyone calls..."

"Mr. Grant." David raised his hand, silencing her. "My apologies, Mr. Grant. Forgive my loquacious daughter. I'm glad to see you're still here. Considering my offer?"

"Abel."

"Of course. So, this is a yes?"

"It's a developing maybe."

Curious, David gestured for Livia to get out of the two-person Mule. He saw the protest on her face. "We won't have our guest, or you, sitting in a filthy cargo bed." She begrudgingly complied, stepping out of the vehicle. David slid over and took the wheel. "Please, join me... Abel."

Abel sat beside his host, climbing over a wide fender flare to reach the passenger seat. Behind them, the small cargo area held a toolbox, loose wood slats, and a coil of rope, all dusted with dirt and sitting in a dried puddle of oil. Abel knew Livia likely wouldn't have minded sitting back there if it meant being included in the family business and spending more time with him, but he understood why David objected. The man barely tolerated his daughter's tomboyishness and would have had a conniption at seeing her carefree and smeared in old motor oil before a guest.

David drove Abel through the seemingly endless vineyard, down the twisting trail that cut through the fields. As Abel took in the beautiful countryside, David could tell the sight of the surrounding hills lined with rows of vines impressed him.

"You're looking at 130 acres of the finest berries to ever grace a bottle," David said. "Each acre holds nearly 3,000 vines, giving us roughly 350,000 altogether."

"Your estate is as bountiful as it is beautiful."

"How poetic. Can I put that on our brochures?"

"Please do," Abel said, not sure if David was being earnest or sarcastic. With David's consistent, stern tone and penchant for business, he realized it could be both.

"Everyone becomes a poet when they remark on how pretty and tranquil Della Luna is, how colorful the trees look in blossom season, how inviting the trails appear as they wind into the hills. I understand their awe, but I grew up here. I've seen the trees and the blooms and the sunsets thousands of times. It's only during harvest, when the vines are full and the berries are ripe, as they are now, only then do I take notice. I craft wine, not prose or postcards."

"I like to think it's our lives that we craft," Abel said, "every moment of every day, and what a life you've crafted here."

David nodded, always appreciating when someone saw the hard work behind his stunning property. "Enough about the blossoms. Tell me about 'developing maybe.'"

"You said Livia would make a good salesperson. I think Rosemary could also join your sales team."

"Agreed," David said with a smile. "My wife could convince a vagabond in winter to hand over his only coat."

"I'd been determined to leave, but after speaking with her... I have a thought I'd like to share with you."

"I can't wait."

"As you know, I don't accept money."

"Yes, something most foreign to me."

"The Community United Church of the Beloved Saint Nelia. Downtown."

David nodded, familiar with the church. He laughed, figuring out where Abel's proposal was heading.

"Become their benefactor," Abel said. "Help them update their shelter, catch up on bills, bring them up to code. It's good work for any man. Do this and I'll stay the week."

"I see. From what I've seen of that church, I'm guessing we're talking somewhere mid five figures?"

"Likely."

"For a man who won't accept money, you're very expensive. I'm only asking for a few more days. Is it worth that much to have you around?"

"Ask Rosemary. Ask Miguel."

"Yes, and Rodrigo."

David stopped the Blue Mule at a barn far from the other buildings.

"Is this where you bottle your wines?" Abel asked.

David shut off the engine and turned to his guest. "Yes, but let's finish our business first."

"So, you are familiar with the church?"

"Good ol' St. Nelia's. Been a while. I was baptized there, attended a few weddings, my uncle's funeral. No need to bargain with me, I'll gladly donate."

"In exchange for another two days."

"Two or three, depending on how things go."

"Two or three," Abel said, hiding his hesitation.

"Good. Now we shake hands."

"There is one other thing I ask while I stay on your property."

"Name it."

"I have an assistant."

* * *

Two hours later, Livia sat in the kitchen, halfway through her lunch of eggs and potatoes, when she heard the doorbell chime. She walked to the entry and opened the door, not expecting to see a scary stone-faced gangster towering above her, carrying a duffel bag.

Carlos looked around, as if memorizing every detail of the grounds and house.

"You're the guy?" Livia asked. "Abel's assistant?"

"Is that what he fuckin' calls me?"

"What should we fuckin' call you?"

Carlos saw Abel walking down the central hall toward them. He sighed in relief at the welcome sight of his boss. "'The guy' will do."

"At ease, Big Man. This is Livia. No need to watch her."

Carlos felt unsure, but nodded that he understood.

"So, you guys are makin' lists, yeah?" Livia asked. "Who to watch and who's alright?"

"Carlos is."

"Nothing personal," Carlos said.

"I guess I can cross you off my watch list, too," Livia said.

Carlos betrayed a slight smile at Livia's retort as she returned to her eggs and potatoes, leaving the two men at the door.

Abel led Carlos through the house to the rear property and down the trail to the guest house. During their long walk, they talked about Marci's involvement with Mr. Felix and his crew, and Reverend Dean's expansion of the church's Sunday school building. Not a word was spoken about the deal struck with David, both men hesitant to talk business until they were behind a closed door, not trusting the many eyes and ears in the fields they passed.

Carlos stopped at the porch and took in the sight of the massive vineyard. "All this fancy vino, and I'd kill for a Corona."

They entered the guest house, its fine interior on full display in the afternoon light, the sun poking in through heavy, gray clouds.

"Questions?" Abel asked, as he opened a bottle of wine.

"Yeah, I got questions. We can start with 'What the hell are we doing here?'"

"Bellini is going to help St. Nelia fix up the shelter, pay some bills." Abel poured the red wine into a crystal decanter.

"St. Nelia is doin' fine, boss."

"They may have a new Sunday school, but they're always behind on ten other things. Bellini's donation will help a lot."

"For what? Having you as his pet?"

"I saved a few folks here. Turns out the hazards of a vineyard rival the streets."

"This vineyard, maybe."

"It's just a week in paradise," Abel said. "A couple of days for you."

Carlos laughed at the thought of the property being anyone's idea of paradise. He tossed his duffel bag on the couch and took a quick look in the other rooms, like a Secret Service agent clearing the area.

"This Bellini guy worries me, Boss," Carlos said from the bedroom. "He's like Angel Ventana Part Two."

Abel didn't respond. He sat at the dining table and poured a glass of wine from the decanter. He took a sip as he waited for his friend to complete his security sweep.

Carlos returned to the living room and stretched out on the couch like he owned the place. "Got some dirt on those two suits, those meatheads scoping you out at the Queens."

"I already know, they were with Bellini's daughter."

"Nope. Different suits. I seen 'em twice since you took off, followed 'em to the same warehouses where they messed with Marci."

"Where you nearly killed five men, you mean," Abel said.

"You should know, nearly killing men is a helluva lot harder that going full measure, like trying to injure bugs without squashing them."

"I'm proud of you for showing restraint, if not mercy."

"You should also know that entire row of warehouses is run by Brennan, that punyeta that pointed his gun at you. I knew I shoulda shoved his head through a fuckin' window."

Abel sighed in frustration, knowing that his Mexican-Filipino friend only cursed in Tagalog when fear mixed with his usual anger. Rigo's warning suddenly came into focus.

"Tell me."

"So I did some digging," Carlos said. "This Brennan guy's connected all the way up. He ships and stores product for the cartel."

"The man who was crying and begging me for help is a cartel captain?"

"Nah, he ain't made, just important and well paid. From what I can tell, his crew don't know he's a dead man walking. The guy's chest and stomach look like sausage pizza, but he still commands them, got 'em staking out the Queens 24-7."

Abel stood and headed for the door. "Don't confront Brennen's men. Not them, not Bellini's men, no matter what. You follow me?"

Carlos saw how serious Abel was, heard the trace of fear in his voice. He reset his attitude. "You know I follow you, Boss. I'll watch you close like always."

"Forget me. Watch everyone else. Dinner is at dusk, on the patio."

Carlos nodded as Abel walked out the door with a final word. "Drink some wine, Carlos. Learn to like it. It's good for you. And I get the feeling it's an insult around here if you refuse."

Abel walked out, shutting the door behind him. Carlos spotted several bottles of wine on the table, the valuable vintages Rosemary had chosen. He picked up the crystal decanter between them and took a long chug.

# 13

# Trust Between Us

When Asuzcena, one of three maids at the estate, told Rigo that Mr. Bellini wanted to see him in his office, his first thought was that he was being reassigned to the city to keep close watch on Brennan, to monitor the traffic of his shipments. Rigo had long wanted to return to La Fig, as it would give him more time with his mother and sister who still lived in the St. Nelia District.

His immediate second thought was that the cook on the patio had overheard his conversation with Abel and shared it with someone who shared it with someone else. Rigo shrugged off his anxiety. Though rumors spread quickly at the winery, he knew no one dared speak above their station. Chatter among field workers never left the fields. Gossip within the house staff was never shared with anyone not in a domestic uniform. Above all else, if Rigo were to endure David's wrath, it wouldn't be in the middle of the afternoon. Such dressings down always occurred at night, especially if they were followed by visits to the barn or one-way trips to the hills.

When Rigo entered David's office, he saw his boss sitting behind his grand desk, scrutinizing 8x10 photos from a large envelope. He stood at the door until addressed, something he quickly learned upon moving to Della Luna.

"Close the door, Rodrigo," David said, still fixed on the photos.

Rigo shut the door and sat in the chair in front of David's desk. He waited a solid minute before breaking the uncomfortable silence.

"Grant," Rigo said. "How long he stay?"

"He's finishing the week. It'll give us time to see what kind of man he really is."

"He is real," Rigo said, confused. "We seen it."

"Oh yes, we've all seen it, but that's not what's in doubt."

David slid a stack of the photos across his desk to Rigo. Rather than pick them up, Rigo spread them apart on the desktop and looked at them all at once. He saw Brennan outside the Royal Queen Motel, talking to a group of homeless men on Arrowhead Avenue, walking to his Dodge Viper parked outside the church. Other photos showed Carlos and Abel at the motel, eating cheeseburgers near the lowrider Impala, Abel walking home alone at dusk.

Rigo understood the implication, that Abel worked for Brennan in the city, but still shook his head as he gathered the photos in a pile and handed them to David.

"No, the angel work for God," Rigo said.

"I'm not convinced. Hell, even Grant isn't convinced. I ask myself, why would he meet with Brennan? And the very next day, he shows up here?"

"Maybe Brennan sick?"

"Doubtful."

"I don't think..."

"Then let's think now!" David stood and walked around his desk to pace near the door. "Grant convinces my daughter that he's the messiah, then my wife, then the incident with Miguel. After all that, he proposes I sugar-daddy a church... in Brennan's territory."

"Ask him..."

"I'm asking you, Rodrigo! Am I being set up?"

Rigo was uneasy with the course of the conversation. He expected some anguish over Brennan's presence, but had foreseen no notions of a takeover. The two men were heads of their own crews, were former partners, and recent rivals, and it felt far too soon for talk of a gang war.

"If the man has the power to heal," David said, convincing himself more than his trustee, "it stands to reason he also has the power to kill. My next handshake could be my last, while he turns Brennan's crew into supermen." David looked at Rigo for a moment as if to study him, to scan his face for any hesitation. Somehow, Rigo maintained his tough, determined expression without betraying his apprehension. "I'm pampering Mr. Grant, giving him his every desire. I need to see how it plays out. And I need to know where your loyalties lie, Rodrigo. He helped you once, and I respect that, but the page has turned since then. I must feel a strong trust between us, right here, now, and moving forward. You follow me, son?"

Rigo hated his boss's spiral of suspicion and paranoia. He wanted to defend the angel who gave him back his legs, but he knew, as did everyone else under his employ, that once David Bellini made a decision, he could not be dissuaded. He simply nodded and cleared his throat.

"I knew you were a good man, Rodrigo. You may believe in him, but I believe in you. That's the difference. Remember that." David opened the door and gestured for Rigo to exit first. "Come now, there's someone you need to speak with."

David told Rigo to fetch the Blue Mule and drive them to the barn, an order that belied their conversation of renewed trust and loyalty. From his first day working at Della Luna, Rigo knew that only two things happened in that barn on the far north end of the vines. The first purpose of the barn involved packaging, the bottling and boxing of wine and berries. Their new bottling line had just been assembled and had yet to make its maiden shipment. The second purpose of the barn was part of an open secret about David and his greater operation, something Rigo hoped didn't factor into their sudden visit there at sundown.

Rigo parked the utility vehicle in front of the barn next to Miguel's BMW sedan. Seeing the car made him reconsider his relationship with both David and Miguel. Though Rigo felt that he'd earned Miguel's respect, he knew his associate could turn on anyone in seconds if ordered. Rigo again wondered if David knew about his talk with Abel on the patio. As he walked through the barn's side door ahead of his employer, he wanted desperately to run outside and into the hills with the miraculous legs God's Hand had given him and see if they were strong enough to speed him away, to disappear in the dark.

David and Rigo entered the barn and walked past the new bottling equipment, past tall stacks of crates filled with berries ready to be pressed into table wine, and headed into the rear storage room. Miguel stood in the center of the small room in front of a man tied to a metal chair. The man wore jogging clothes and sat beaten bloody, on the verge of passing out. Rigo maintained his tough stone face, hiding his disgust and fear, harboring a sudden and surreal relief that he was not the one in the chair that night.

"Rodrigo, this is Orlando Paz," David said. The exhausted man only sat upright because of the duct tape wrapped around his chest, waist, and lower legs, and around the heavy-gauge steel of the chair. Though his outlook was grim, he glared at Rigo with disdain. "Orlando has been jogging around the vineyards for a couple of weeks." David knelt in front of his captive. "Tell us again why you've been hanging around our hills?"

Orlando looked at David before him, at Miguel standing just behind his boss, and at Rigo near the door. "It's pretty country," he said in defiance. "Nice for a morning run."

"Yes, I agree. I occasionally go for a morning walk through the vines." David stood and turned to Rigo. "It took us a couple of weeks to uncover that Orlando is part of Brennan's crew in La Fig."

"I don't know nothing about that," Orlando said, spitting out a glob of blood.

"Rodrigo, I know that dealing with Grant might be tough for you. It's going to take all your nerve. For now, we have Orlando. This is a grand opportunity. We can send Brennan a message."

Any threads of sympathy Rigo had for the man in the chair evaporated the moment he spoke, giving away his flimsy cover as a tourist and confirming his role as one of Brennan's well-known button men. Though he looked helpless, he was likely one of St. Nelia's enforcers, and had surely strapped many others in his own chair in the city. Rigo's only thought now was to comply, to survive another day in David's good graces.

Rigo reached into his inner coat pocket and pulled out a gun. He walked away from the tempting open doorway and approached their captive, pointing his weapon at Orlando's head. As expected, Orlando didn't beg for his life, didn't flinch, didn't offer a deal. He simply returned Rigo's stare mockingly.

"Why?" Rigo asked him in Spanish. "Why did Brennan send you to spy on us? There's no point in lying, you know how this is going to end. You can at least die with dignity."

"I said I don't know nothing about that," Orlando said in English, firmly repeating his one ready response.

Rigo kept his gun on him, hoping for more, if only to delay the inevitable. David lost patience and grabbed the gun from his trustee. He shot Orlando in the chest and shoved the gun back into Rigo's extended hand.

Rigo quickly returned his gun to his inner coat pocket, hoping the movement would hide his trembling hand. "You didn't need... do that," he said, back to English. "I can do it... for you."

"But you didn't."

"I wanted more... for him to talk."

David let Rigo off the hook, tenderly placing his arm around him. "I know you can do it for me. That's why you're here. I just figured I'd take it off your hands. Take a long look at this man sitting here, Rodrigo. You see now what the angel has brought to our hills? Can I trust you to do the right thing when the time comes?"

Orlando groaned, still barely alive. With David and Miguel on either side of him, Rigo made his decision, convincing himself that he had a choice. He reached for his gun again and in one swing of his arm shot Orlando in the forehead.

"I follow you... boss."

"That's my boy."

# 14

## Stand Up

Abel and Livia stood on the back steps of the patio leading onto the primary trail, looking out over the rear property. Despite the dense clouds that had been gathering over Della Luna for days, the morning was clear enough to allow sight of the bunkhouse, guest house, and barn far in the distance, their rooftops showing above the thousands of rolling vines. Livia had made them both coffee from a newly opened bag of Sumatra beans, freshly ground and brewed only minutes before the pour, offering Abel the finest cup he'd tasted in a decade.

"Forget wine," Abel said, savoring his first sip, followed by a quick second. "You make a mean cup of joe."

"Thanks. I still got a lot to learn about wine, but I'm definitely a bonafide coffee snob. Pop says I get it from my mom."

"She doesn't seem the coffee type. She insisted on tutoring me on the finer points of rare vintages."

"Rosemary is my stepmom, remember? My mom-mom passed away when I was little."

"I'm sorry, Livia," Abel said, treading lightly. "How did she die, if you don't mind me asking?"

"Don't sweat it, I don't mind, but it was... complicated. Let's just say even you couldn't have helped her." Livia sipped her coffee before daring to change the subject with a nagging concern. "You're 'assistant' is certainly interesting."

"Carlos is a good man."

"You for-sure about that?"

"He's the only person on Earth that I am sure about."

"So, you ain't for-sure about me just yet?"

"Smart kid," Abel said as he drank his coffee.

"I heard about Miguel."

"I imagine everyone's heard about Mr. Valencia by now. Does David know? I mean, does he know all the details? The injury, the money, the witnesses."

"Shit, I can't think of anything Pop don't know."

Abel lit a cigarette, barely realizing he'd done so. It became a habit so ingrained in him that the little ritual before each smoke felt almost involuntary. He'd slam the pack into his left palm three times, slide a cigarette out while readying his lighter, lit it while pocketing the pack, and shut his eyes with the first slow drag. He often went through an entire pack of White Knights on auto-pilot before startling himself by reaching into an empty box, his heavy habit sneaking up on him again.

His every cigarette came and went without notice, for Abel always had other things on his mind, and at that moment his most pressing thoughts were of Miguel and David. The cover story of Miguel getting impaled by a pitchfork seemed flimsy but passable, but Abel wondered if Rigo had told his boss about the bullets he'd pulled from his associate, and how the estate's master would react to his second life being exposed.

Livia scooted away, wincing at the smell of the cigarette. "First smoke of the day?" Abel held up three fingers as he took another drag. "Damn, the rooster crows and you're already lighting up Number Three. I guess lung cancer don't really apply to you, yeah?"

"Can't heal myself, remember?"

"So you hurt yourself instead?"

"Smart kid," Abel said with a slight smile. "What does your father think about that night?"

"The night with Miguel? Pop would say it goes with the territory. You get hurt on a farm, especially during crunch time. But he cares. That's why he wants you here, yeah?"

"I wonder about that, Livia. I worked on a farm when I was a boy. Potatoes, onions, and corn. Twelve-hour days in the sun. It was hard labor, but even on our toughest days we didn't need a miracle worker on retainer."

"It's good to be over-prepared, I suppose."

"What happens when a real worker gets hurt? I'm talking the men in the fields. A lot of them are in constant pain, from dawn well into the night. They try to hide it, every torn muscle, every blown knee, every busted back. I feel it all, even now, as we stand here with our gourmet coffees and pleasant chit-chat. Does your pop care about them?"

Livia hesitated, not sure how to respond. "S'yeah, 'course he does. He cares about all those guys."

"You for-sure about that?"

Livia felt insulted, though she realized she'd questioned his judgement a moment before, setting loose the first arrow of suspicion toward Abel's trusted guardian. Their conversation halted when they spotted a Mercedes-Benz sedan arrive across the property, parking beside the manor. Three men in pristine suits and polished shoes stepped out of the car and headed for the house. The luxury car and formal attire contrasted with their rustic surroundings and the talk of hard labor in a vineyard.

Abel watched the trio enter the house. "I think the real reason I'm here is to care for men who wear Armani suits and drive fancy cars, men who mysteriously get impaled by pitchforks in the middle of the night. It goes against my mission. I'm devoted to the less fortunate."

"If you really feel that way, why the hell are we standing here with our gourmet coffees?"

"You're right." Abel eyed the Blue Mule parked nearby. "Got keys to that thing?"

* * *

Livia drove Abel into the vineyard to a group of field workers harvesting grapes. It looked like back-breaking work, bent over with buckets for hours, the sun beating down on them through gaps in the dense clouds. Miguel stood a short distance away, near a work truck, supervising them as he popped pills from a small plastic bottle. He walked to the utility vehicle, amused to see Abel again.

"Curandero!" Miguel said, his arm outstretched. "Good morning!"

"Headaches, Mr. Valencia?" Abel said, eyeing the pill bottle. Miguel quickly pocketed the pills and walked to the workers. "You should know, pills won't help."

"You don't know these pills."

The workers turned in awe as they noticed Abel entering the vines with Livia and Miguel.

"What I know is that your head will pound and your hands will shake. You'll feel ice cold. You won't be able to think straight as you slowly go mad, and it will all get worse unless you pay me."

Miguel laughed through his growing agony. "That fat roll wasn't enough? I mean, I don't remember that cash being brought back to me. Damn, you are good, Curandero!"

"Fuck off, Miguel," Livia said.

The field workers looked beat. Two of them walked to a large water cooler on the tailgate of the truck. Miguel blocked their path, denying them as if to show Livia the difference between a boss and a boss's daughter. He spoke to the workers in Spanish. "Nope. Lunch is in three hours. You can drown in a bucket then."

Abel walked up to the water cooler, but was stopped by Miguel's hand covering the spigot.

"For you or for them?" Miguel asked in English.

"I'm not the one dying in a field."

"That's what I thought. These guys ain't dying, they had plenty when they started."

"That was hours ago." Abel felt their clawing thirst.

"Let them work. Coming over here will kill their rhythm."

"Then I'll bring water to them. They won't stop working."

"No, but they'll start expecting. We go soft on them, they go soft on the job."

Abel looked out at the defeated faces of the field workers. "My job is to help them."

"No one's bleeding on the bunkhouse floor last I checked, Curandero."

"He ain't talkin' break time!" Livia said. "Just give 'em a fuckin' drink!"

Miguel shot her a stern look before clutching his head in pain from what felt like a hammer to his temple. He knelt down beside the cooler and took a long drink from the spigot, to both calm his nerves and flex his authority. He picked up the cooler and carried it to a nearby SUV, setting it in the passenger seat. Miguel struggled to walk around the car and sit behind the wheel, panting, clinching his eyes tight.

Abel watched Miguel's growing torment, compounded by his stubborn refusal to listen. He walked into the vines and joined the field workers. He gestured for everyone to gather around him, to hold hands in a circle. Some knelt and bowed their heads in prayer.

"No, stand up," Abel said in Spanish. "Always stand."

The workers no longer felt parched. They seemed renewed, thankful for the respite. They all shook Abel's hand before promptly returning to their work. Livia watched from afar, speechless.

Now exhausted, Abel strained to reach the SUV. He whipped open the passenger door and desperately gulped water from the cooler. Miguel offered no resistance as he clutched the steering wheel, weak, desperate to breathe.

The familiar sight of Miguel pressed against the wheel took hold of Abel, triggering a memory that normally stormed him in dreams.

# 15

# In The Mud

A full moon shone over the Devil's Backbone, lighting the tops of the Sumacs, Cedar Elms, Red Maples, and the limestone embankment that Regina drove off of hours before. Trying to avoid colliding with another car on the lonely cliffside road, she sent Abel's Corvette roaring through the air into the thick branches of an old Live Oak at the bottom of a ravine, the ancient tree looking like a giant mossy hand emerging from the earth, gripping the sports car like a toy.

With Phillip Crescenzo's grand birthday celebration over, its last lingering guests saying their late-night goodbyes, the talent agent wondered where his star client and her gifted husband had vanished to. He made several calls to both of the Grants, but no cell phone signal reached that desolate ravine. Knowing how much that evening meant to Regina, to perform before the crème de la crème of the music industry, Phillip feared the worst. He left messages on their voice mail, called every hospital between Austin and San Antonio, and asked guests to update him should any of them encounter their mutual friends. Of all the dark scenarios running through his mind, Phillip could never have imagined the Grants trapped in a tree all night near Canyon Lake.

Regina opened her eyes again and struggled to breathe, the steering wheel pressed into her chest as she barely clung to life. Abel sat on a branch beside the car, unable to reach her or make a phone call. He sat dumbfounded, knowing he needed to somehow climb the steep embankment and return to the road hoping to get a cell signal or flagging down a passing car, but he feared leaving his wife's side. He imagined returning to find that she'd departed from this world, alone in the wreckage.

He saw her eyes drifting to sleep again.

"Hold on, baby! You can't doze off! Not now! You gotta hold on!" Abel rubbed the crucifix on his necklace.

"The other car," Regina said, moaning, speaking in slow exhales.

"What?"

"The other car... are they... okay?"

"Who gives a shit about them! They forced you off the road! They're probably halfway to Phoenix by now!"

"No," Regina said. "I saw them go down... like us."

"Serves them right!"

Regina breathed heavily as she strained to talk. "My bad driving... didn't help. Go to them..."

"I'm staying put till help arrives." Abel sounded firm, though he knew the odds of anyone noticing them in the ravine was slim. He rubbed his crucifix again and silently prayed.

"Don't... pray for me," Regina said. "I'll be fine."

"I know you will, but The Lord must know it was my fault! I drank too much! It's why you drove. You can't drive stick. It should be me stuck in there!"

"Check... the other car..."

Torn about leaving his wife, he looked around until he spotted the lights of the other car down the ravine, wrecked along the embankment.

"I don't care about them," Abel said firmly, "but I'll have a look if that's really want you want."

Regina nodded.

It would be the last thing she'd ever ask of him.

Abel started the difficult climb down the tree.

Abel awoke, disoriented and startled to find himself in the full-size bed of the estate's guest house. The recurring nightmare had placed him back in that dark ravine almost nightly for ten years, each dream feeling like he'd traveled back in time to relive every minute of the worst night of his life. He wished that the memory would fade, yet felt grateful that he still had a perfect recollection of his wife's peaceful face and wavering voice, as pained as it was.

He rose from bed and wandered into the living room where Carlos snored on the sofa, his long legs dangling off the side. Moonlight beamed onto the large wooden crucifix on the wall, and Abel couldn't bear to look at it. He turned away, toward the front door, just as a soft knock grabbed his attention. He considered waking his friend but allowed him his rest as he answered the door, opening it a few inches.

Abel didn't know who to expect at such a late hour, but would have never pictured Rosemary standing in the doorway in a wool coat over her night dress.

"Mrs. Bellini?"

"Mr. Grant. May I come in?"

Abel glanced at Carlos, still sound asleep. "I don't think that's a good idea. The Big Man gets cranky if he's woken up."

"Well, it is a lovely night."

Abel took his coat from a nearby hook and joined Rosemary on the porch, carefully shutting the door behind him. They sat on a wooden bench in silence, admiring the view of the moonlit vineyard and distant mansion. Abel reached into his coat and pulled out his White Knights, lighting up a smoke. Rosemary gave him a moment.

"I need your help again," she said after allowing him a couple of drags.

"How are you feeling? Any pain?"

"No, no, that's gone, like the disease was ripped from my body. I'm sure you know the feeling."

"It leaves me drained, nauseous, but I don't really know what you go through, how you feel."

"I suppose you couldn't know. Livia says you can't heal yourself."

"I've been told it feels like weeds being pulled from a garden," Abel said.

"More like a chicken being plucked for Sunday Supper."

"I've heard something like that, too. I suppose the experience is different for each person." Abel took another drag from his cigarette and peered into the vines, looking for someone, for anyone. They seemed to be alone.

"Tell me."

"I want to leave this life," Rosemary said. "Leave the farm."

"It doesn't take a miracle to walk away from a marriage."

"It does with this one."

"And you think I can help somehow?"

"I confess, I know more about you than David does. I know about the motel and the church, and that bad bit of business in Texas. My apologies for ransacking your past." Rosemary saw the subtle surprise on his face. "Who do you think told Livia how to find you?"

"So much for her 'detective work.' How long have you wanted out?"

"Since Livia was on two feet. I want out now, while I'm still on mine."

Abel stood and paced the front of the porch, again looking around to ensure no one was watching or listening. "That isn't why I'm here."

"Isn't it? God sent you to save me. So save me. You took away the cancer, now you must take me away."

"Please understand..."

"Have your man look up Eliza Bellini, David's first wife, Livia's mother. She died in the vines, not far from here. "

"What would I discover?"

"Eliza had an affair with a mechanic and was found face-down in the mud." Abel could only stare at her as he processed her blunt reveal, unable to respond. "He'd been having an affair of his own, so he married his mistress."

"And now the mistress sits here beside me and wants to run away before she also finds herself in the mud. Is that it?"

Desperate, Rosemary threw away caution and laid the entire truth before him. "David surely had his men take care of the mechanic, but I'm certain he took care of Eliza himself. I know him too well."

Abel had always hated the phrase "take care of" in place of murder, just as he'd always hated "passed away" in place of death. Sugar-coating such acts did nothing to ease his revulsion, sorrow, and guilt.

"Does Livia feel that way?" he asked.

"She was just a child. She thinks the mechanic did it. But a wife, even a second wife, knows her husband better than a daughter knows her father."

"That was long ago. After all this time, why now?"

Rosemary couldn't say the words, but Abel didn't need to hear them. He gripped her hand and felt her anguish, her overwhelming desire to flee with another. He felt love and compassion within her, and assumed it was concern for Livia in her mind. The realization then hit him immediately.

"Dr. Flowers..."

"Forget her," Rosemary said. "It's you I need. I know that now."

"Rosemary, it's not that simple."

"I want to take Livia with me. Perhaps you can tell her, show her the truth. Better it comes from you."

Abel tossed his cigarette into the dirt and sat beside Rosemary on the bench. "That's not how it works."

"Then explain to me, how does it work?" Her voice trembled in desperation. "Tell me what to do."

"Return to your glorious house, your extravagant life. Think about exactly what you want. I have some thinking to do as well, but my first thought is that whatever you decide, you're on your own, or we'll all be in the mud."

Rosemary wiped away a tear. Without another word, she stood and headed down the long trail back to the manor.

Abel went back into the dark guest house to find Carlos awake, kneeling on the sofa by the front window, having just overheard the entire conversation.

"You want me to look up that woman like she said?" Carlos asked.

"Doesn't matter. She's telling the truth."

"What we gonna do, Boss?"

Exasperated, Abel sat on the sofa beside his friend. "This could spiral out of our hands."

"Ain't it already? Shit, we shoulda never left the Queens."

"That wouldn't have mattered, either."

The two men sat in silence, pondering their next move.

Twenty-two minutes later, Rosemary reached the manor and quietly made her way into the house. She didn't notice David sitting on the rear patio, watching her from the shadows, as he had been for the past hour. As she walked upstairs, David remained outside, staring out at the distant guest house.

# 16

## Payment

The following morning, Abel took a long, hot shower, a simple luxury he'd never had at the North Star Arms. A selection of French-milled soap and flowery shampoo Livia had arranged gave his bathroom the feel of a five-star resort. The hazelnut and shea butter conditioner she chose would remain unused since Abel's thinning hair receded more each day and Carlos regularly shaved his head, but its faux antique bottle sat on the sink as a nice decoration.

Abel turned the shower knob counterclockwise until the water flowed as hot as he could get it, almost scalding, an attempt to wash away another vivid nightmare with both soap and shocking pain. The detailed dreams of Regina trapped in the ravine had been occurring more often, sometimes several nights in a row, to such a degree that Abel often remained lucid. He treasured being "awake" in those dreams, for he could take in the beauty of his wife's face and voice once more, even as he knew the unavoidable outcome. It also served as a reminder of how powerless he was until that last cruel moment.

Carlos made a carafe of coffee in the kitchen while he waited for his turn in the deluxe shower. He was both impressed and overwhelmed by a guest house, a living space more ornate, appointed, and comfortable than any home he'd ever known. After living at the Royal Queen Motel for years, and at similar abandoned properties before, the Bellini estate seemed breathtaking almost to a fault. The manicured grounds and sterling buildings nearly suffocated him. He told himself that he actually missed the tagged cinderblock walls and background traffic noise of the St. Nelia District.

After the coffee machine beeped, and Carlos poured two cups, he admitted to himself that the real reason he pined for his inner-city borough was because of his status within that struggling urban community. On Arrowhead Avenue and the adjacent H Street, Carlos Cruz was the proverbial big fish in the small pond. Everyone on the streets knew his name and either feared or respected him. At Della Luna, he still felt like a big fish, now swimming in a beautiful tank full of sharks.

Abel came out of the bedroom refreshed and fully dressed. He joined his guardian at the dining table, picked up his awaiting coffee, and lit his first cigarette of the day.

"What's on the clipboard?" Carlos asked, a question he posed each morning when Reverend Dean arrived at the motel at dawn with a new list of visitors to expect.

"I'm here to help the workers," Abel said. "I'm heading back into the fields."

"Ain't you helped them enough?"

"Not yet." Abel took a moment to savor his coffee. "Good stuff, Big Man. I could get used to this."

"Don't."

"I know. We'll be back at the Queens soon, and I'll be back to choking down the reverend's burnt sludge."

"This place, this 'paradise' as you say, it ain't our world, Boss."

Abel looked at his friend and laughed at how he threw his former choice of words back at him. "I realized a long time ago that paradise isn't a location. It's not green hills or colorful flowers or fine wine. It's not nestled in rolling hills or an endless garden or behind golden gates in the clouds. Paradise is love. It's good people. Better to be in a dying wasteland with those you care about than in the Promised Land with folks who just want to exploit you, discard you."

"You should write the reverend's sermons," Carlos said with a smirk. "He talks about the Kingdom of Heaven like it's Disneyland for Christians, and all you gotta do is behave yourself while you wait in line for a ticket."

"Reverend Dean is a good man, Carlos."

"A good man can still be a fool. They usually are."

"As are we."

Carlos sat silent, holding his warm coffee cup with two hands, the rising run shining through the kitchen's bay window onto their table. He didn't need to verbally agree with his boss, for Abel knew they'd both seen their private paradises fade away, never to return, at around the same time ten years before.

"Be honest with me, Boss. Is either of us ever seein' paradise again?"

"I believe we will. But there's a cost, and we'll be paying for the rest of our lives, with what we do with our lives."

Carlos took in his boss's words. He thought about his criminal past, at all those he hurt for personal gain, and concluded that for all his hustling and posturing and obsessing over territory, he ended up as just another blight on other people's lives, a blemish in their paradise. He knew his road to redemption would be long and likely without end. It put their shared mission into sharp focus, like a bracer for another morning in those treacherous hills.

Carlos slammed his coffee and headed to the bathroom for his turn in the luxurious shower. Abel took another moment to finish his cup before taking his smoke outside. He started down the long path from the guest house south to the manor, but found himself drawn to the shorter path north into the fields.

He cut across the vines and walked to a group of field workers picking grapes and dumping them into a nearby truck. Once again, they were supervised by Miguel, his impeccable suit mocking their harsh labor. As before, he popped pills in agony, failing to hide his intense pain when he saw Abel approaching.

"Be straight with me, Curandero," Miguel said in a hoarse voice. "What the fuck is happening to me?"

"Tell me."

"I got headaches 24 hours. My skin itches like bugs crawling all over. I thought you was a healer?"

"I don't see you bleeding on the bunkhouse floor, Mr. Valencia."

"Yeah, but what about all this other shit?"

"You still haven't paid me."

Despite their lowered voices, heads turned in the field, the workers hearing the conflict between the two men.

"I don't appreciate you making me look like a chump."

Before Abel could again remind the stubborn man of his obligation, an older field worker dropped his harvest bucket and collapsed to the ground. He clutched his chest, struggling to breathe.

"Get up!" Miguel said, barking his order. "You ain't gettin' paid to take a nap!"

Abel walked to the worker and helped him to his feet. They held hands for a moment before the old man nodded and returned to his bucket. Abel returned to Miguel by the truck.

"You really like doing that, don't you?" Miguel said, shaking his head. "You like playing the saint, making me out to be the bad guy."

"I can't control how people see you, Mr. Valencia. Only you can do that."

"How fuckin' deep. Save that shit for a bumper sticker."

"And David wants to keep these men going. What would you have me do?"

Miguel forced a laugh, even as he pinched the bridge of his nose to quash his throbbing pain. "You have no clue what 'David' wants. But you will. Till then, just hang around like a walking, talking rabbit's foot, and stay the hell out of my way."

"Take it easy, Mr. Valencia."

"I'll make this as simple as I can. Don't test me and don't tell me how to run my men. Angel or whatever, I will make a fuckin' example of you. You see, that's what I do for 'David.'"

Carlos stood behind the truck, having heard everything. He'd cut his shower short when he heard the door of the guest house slam shut as Abel left. He walked up to Miguel and stared at him, inches from his pained face. "Don't be threatening Mr. Grant."

"Who the fuck are you?" Miguel asked.

"Don't you know? I'm the guy you heard about."

"Yeah, now that you mention it, I did hear about a big fucker lurking around. Since when does a holy man need a bodyguard?"

"Since men like you is around. So I'll say it again, and I'll make it as simple as I can, don't be threatening Mr. Grant."

"Or what?"

"Or I'll make an example of you."

Miguel noticed the many eyes from the vines. "So, it's like that? Well, now I'm threatening both of you. This is my world, not yours."

"Agreed," Carlos said. "But if you and me go 'round and 'round, even he won't be able to put you back together."

Miguel and Carlos faced each other like two schoolyard bullies jockeying for dominance. Abel halted the scene by grabbing Miguel's hand. For a moment, Miguel expected something to happen, for Abel's touch to take away the constant ache that pounded him. He felt disappointed when the pain never subsided.

"Don't focus on him, Miguel," Abel said. "Pay me. Something you've made. I don't care what it is. It's how this works."

Miguel briefly thought about what he could offer, but quickly dismissed the motion, sticking to his conviction that the required payment was just another layer of bullshit, another attempt to chip away at his authority. Perhaps if Abel had pulled the man aside and explained the tradition in private, they might have shared an understanding, but Miguel never offered the chance, seeing compromise and compliance as weakness.

Miguel yanked his arm away from Abel's grip and headed into the vines, leaving him and Carlos by the truck.

"What the hell was that about?" Carlos asked.

"I tried to heal him just now, but he's lived with it too long."

"Lived with what?"

"Anger, fear, contempt, disregard. It's all part of him now." Abel led Carlos away from the workers, back to the guest house.

"If you can't heal sociopaths," Carlos said, "I guess it means I wasn't such a lost cause after all."

"You never were, Big Man." Abel looked back at the men in the field, at Miguel lording over them. He thought about the passive threat he'd made, hinting that David harbored a hidden agenda.

* * *

"I think we're just about done here," Abel said as they reached the porch of the guest house.

Carlos looked confused, torn. "I thought we was staying another day at least?"

"I thought so, too." Abel looked at his friend, surprised to see him mildly frustrated by the news. "I figured you'd be overjoyed to go home."

"I am, but... I heard about a poker game they got going on at the bunkhouse, kinda told those old vaqueros I'd drop by, check it out."

As they entered the guest house, Abel remained fixed on Carlos, sensing his feelings almost as clear as spelled out thoughts. "They remind you of family."

"One of 'em reminds me of Lino, yeah, and this one old dude looks like my tatay."

"Then, by all means, join the game. How often do you get to do something like that?"

"Forget it. I should stick close to you. You're pickin' up on something..."

"It's fine. Play cards, relax, have fun, and hand out Reverend Dean's number. Tell them to contact him if they ever need us."

Carlos regretted mentioning the card game, knowing that Abel would kindly encourage him despite sensing something sinister coming around the corner. He felt selfish, placing his entertainment above their mission, even for only a couple of hours, but the promise of male bonding had a pull on him.

Holding court over a table full of men, tossing down money and dirty jokes and Straight Flushes, was something he missed from his glory days with his old gang. The way those laborers made him think of the Cruz household from his childhood proved too much to ignore.

"Maybe just a couple of hours." Carlos heeded his boss's nudge and opened the door to leave. "Hey, why don't you come with me? I know you don't gamble, but I'd be good to see you relax a little, too."

"Everyone will be more at ease if I'm not there. Besides, I need to speak with David."

"To tell him what?"

"That we're leaving tonight."

Shortly after nightfall, Abel entered David's office, finding him working at his desk, hovered over his computer.

"Good evening, David."

"Mr. Grant... I mean, Abel... please come in. I have good news for you."

"That's always welcome. And I have news for..."

"I'm about to send your payment to that account, for whoever that is."

"You know who it's for."

"The church. Yes, of course. Good thing you caught me here. I'm about to go out for the evening, for a chateaubriand and a pitcher of martinis. How does this amount sit with you?" David swiveled his computer monitor around for Abel to see. The staggering dollar amount at the top of the screen grabbed his attention. "I did my due diligence, estimated what they'll need to meet city code, catch up on bills, and this is what I came up with. Is it satisfactory?"

"More than enough."

"Good. I actually set up the transfer days ago. Now, I only need to hit 'Confirm.'"

Abel waited for him to press the button, but sensed tension in the pause, as if the lingering moment was meant to taunt him. "Hard to part with it?"

"Not at all," David said. "Payment as promised. You are family now, so says Livia." After holding his index finger above the computer's mouse another few seconds, David clicked the button, approving the transfer. "I make that much in an hour. I'm not boasting, I just don't want you to feel it's excessive. You've done me a great service. I now realize things... I'd been blind to."

Abel found their exchange odd. As he pondered the catch to the generous donation, David walked to his wall-length wine rack. He browsed the hundreds of bottles before him.

"But money doesn't close our deal, right?" David asked. "You need something I made, and I certainly made these." He pulled out a bottle and handed it to Abel.

"La Donna Tempesta," Abel said. "We meet again."

"This wine, a man is lucky just to taste it. You've tasted it, shared it with its creator, and now have your very own bottle to do with as you wish... for better or worse."

Abel accepted the rare vintage, examining its exquisite label, a detailed drawing of a silhouetted, faceless queen standing tall in a dense rainstorm, her arms open wide. The macabre image seemed to fit with David's curious warning. "How ominous. Is there a legend?"

"A curse, some say. I made it for my first wife, Eliza. Livia's mother. It was our anniversary." David readied two glasses and continued to look through his wall rack. "Eliza chose the berries, drew that label you gaze at, and even came up with the name. She died the night we tasted it. Brain aneurysm."

"My apologies."

"Found her out in the fields at dawn. She always enjoyed watching the sun shine through the vines. I take solace in knowing that the last thing she saw was that sunrise."

Abel hid his apprehension. He slid his glass across the table and offered his newly gifted bottle to his host. David smiled as he took it back.

"My son Piero," David said as he opened the wine and quickly poured it into a decanter, the rapid sloshing aerating the vintage. "Sixteenth birthday. He broke into my office, bragged about La Donna's price tag, and shared a bottle with friends. We had harsh words and he ran off with them late at night. They took him skinny dipping in Arroyo Grande Creek. Cops dragged his body out three days later."

"I'm so sorry, David."

After giving it a minute to breathe, David poured two glasses of the supposedly cursed wine. "Rosemary opened a bottle and was bed ridden that week. Livia took a sip and had... strange thoughts. She blamed me for everything, as if I could conjure cancer. She started cutting herself, started seeing her mother's ghost walk the halls. I had the girl committed for a year." He handed Abel a glass and the two men shared their first sips. "What do you make of all that?"

"If I were a superstitious man, I'd say that everyone who's tasted this wine was shown death's door. But I'm not a superstitious man."

David smiled as he savored the infamous vintage. "Neither am I. Superstition is for the ignorant and gullible. Still, I wondered. I am the head of this family, after all. Perhaps I was responsible? Perhaps I'm just one tragedy away from seeing the dead roaming the halls myself. So, I chose not to sell this."

"Your masterpiece, your legacy, and you've never sold it?"

"Even tagged at ten-grand a bottle, I had buyers waiting. But now, the greatest vintage that's ever come from this soil, I reserve it for special guests. Only you and I have tasted it since."

Abel had come to announce his departure that evening and felt determined to return to his news before diving deeper into the man's haunted past. "David, what you are is a generous man. I speak for the wine, the money, and your hospitality. But I believe my work here is done. We're heading back to the city tonight. Thank you for taking us into your home." Abel placed his empty glass on the desk and walked to the open door.

David held his glass to the light, observing its color and body. He'd heard his guest's decision but refused to accept it. "There was also poor Raymond."

Abel stopped at the door and turned to face David, whose sudden words and deadpan tone landed with precision.

"He was my lead mechanic, Mr. Grant. You might have heard about him?"

"I might have." Abel sensed that David's return to formal names signaled a shift in their conversation, a grab for control.

"He got his shirt sleeve caught in a well drill. Ripped off his right arm, along with a good portion of his ribcage. Such a loss. He was like family."

Abel knew where David was heading. "Did poor Raymond also fall victim to the curse? Did he have a glass of La Donna Tempesta?"

"He tasted it on Eliza's lips."

Trying to remain calm, Abel simply looked at his host. "Fortunately, we're not superstitious men."

"Whatever you intend to do with that money, Mr. Grant, I suggest you do it quickly. Money comes and money goes, just like good intentions. Just like family."

"Are you still going out tonight?"

"Looks like we both are."

David took his coat from around his chair, put it on, and joined Abel at the doorway, gesturing for his guest to exit first. The two men entered the hall together, David leaving through the front door while Abel returned to the guest house to gather his things and find Carlos.

# 17

# Full House

Carlos sat on a crate in the bunkhouse, up against a large makeshift table comprising three barrels with discarded planks of wood nailed atop. The planks had been sanded and crudely cut to an imperfect circle, just enough time and care for an impromptu poker night. Five field workers sat with him, with another three just behind them, watching the action. Four others lay in their beds listening to the upbeat accordions and rhythmic pattering drums of Tejano music on a single-speaker portable radio.

Engaged in conversation with a room full of Mexican farm laborers, having enjoyed three Corona Light beers and two poker wins since he joined them, Carlos was firmly in his element. As an old man across from him shuffled the cards, Carlos tossed a Hundred onto the table. "I hope that's not too rich for you hard-working men," he said in Spanish. "I need some excitement here in paradise."

Pablo Montez, a 60-year-old man with leathery skin, dressed in cotton thermals and a straw hat, finished his shuffle and dealt a new hand. His slow, enunciated Spanish reminded Carlos of his grandfather. "You're from the city, right? I won't ask you what gang, but your tattoos say you were high up in La Fig."

"All the way up. First Lieutenant."

"Shit, I'm gonna watch out for you, my friend," Pablo said in his soft rural drawl, almost slurring. "Nobody fucks with a First."

"I think you're the one to watch, old man. You won four rounds since I walked in here."

"Of course. I been playing the game longer. You got muscle and you got balls, but I got experience, my friend. Experience and a little luck."

"So that's the secret to winning poker?" Carlos said with a laugh, amused by the old man.

"That, and you always sit with your back to the wall."

"Shit, I do that whether or not I'm playing cards."

"I knew you were a wise man, my friend." Pablo grinned. "I knew it and I told everybody the big fucker isn't as dumb as he looks."

Laughter spread across the workers, rising to a pitch when they saw Carlos laughing along with them.

Javier Manriquez, a third of Pablo's age and overflowing with ten times the energy, laughed the hardest. More than anyone else in that bunkhouse, Javier viewed Carlos's unexpected arrival with excitement, for he'd rarely met anyone from the city - other than old Pablo - who spoke more than five words to him. Somewhat starstruck, he never imagined sitting down for beers and cards with the intimidating guardian of God's Hand.

"How does a First Lieutenant get out of the game like that?" Javier asked, recalling the details of Pablo's past life on the streets. He popped the cork on a large bottle of tequila and lined up five shot glasses. "How did you end up here in the shit with us?"

Pablo slapped the back of Javier's head for being so blunt. "You must forgive Javi. He means no disrespect. I've told him a lot of my stories from my time running with the Nine Kings in La Fig."

"You were BC-9?" Carlos asked, surprised that this gentle old field worker once belonged to the most notorious gang in La Figueira. "What the hell were you doing with them?"

"Living in fear," Pablo said. "I saw my brothers getting shot down or locked away one-by-one. I got out by packing my shit one night and driving up the highway. Simple as that. I worked my way up the coast, doing this and that, whatever needed to be done, until I settled here with these fools. But all that nonsense was a long time ago. Trust me, my friend, it's better out here."

"Most of the time," Javier said, as he poured shots of tequila for all five players, reaching across the table to hand Carlos his. "Can't say that about the bosses. They brought the barrio to paradise, if that's what we're calling it."

Pablo shot the young man a stern look, silencing him, but he'd piqued Carlos's curiosity.

"What's that mean?" Carlos asked.

"It means nothing," Pablo said, humming along with the Tejano music. "The boy just talks too much."

"If it might affect my boss, I need to know."

"It ain't just wine and roses up here," Pablo said, hesitant. "Bellini runs a crew no different than yours or mine back in the day. But you're a wise man, you figured that out by now, right? And some gringo in the city has his own men."

"Boss fucking hates that guy," Javier said, shooting his tequila and promptly pouring another.

"Who's the man in the city?" Carlos asked.

"I don't know names, but Javi's right, Bellini hates him. I hope the gringo doesn't kill us one night on his way to Bellini. You see, First Lieutenant, even out here in the hills, sometimes there's still a gang war."

"There's always a gang war," Carlos said. He realized who the gringo was as the old man dealt a new hand. "And to answer your question, I got out because I'm cursed. People die around me. Four in one night, three were our brothers, all dead because of me. My work with the angel helps me live with that."

The cards remained face-down on the table as Pablo led the workers in raising their glasses out of respect, a toast to their honored guest. The tender moment halted when they noticed five men in suits - Miguel, Rigo, and three more of Bellini's associates - standing at the open doorway.

"Hello again, Carlos," Miguel said in Spanish. "Carlos Joaquin Cruz of the Franklin Heights Guerreros."

The field workers sat silent as Miguel read names from a small notepad, feigning sympathy. "Ozzy Castillo. Ignacio Valle. Lino Cruz. Such a tragic loss. Lino was your nephew, yes? Don't know the fourth corpse." He walked into the room, into the group of onlookers standing near the table. "We can talk here in front of them, but 'people always die around you.' It's why you became the angel's bitch."

Carlos rose to his feet, towering over everyone. "Don't you think of hurtin' no one here."

"Or what?" Miguel asked in defiance. He looked back at his men, ready for anything. "You gonna make an example of me?"

"Let 'em walk out before we do this."

Miguel snorted a laugh and considered Carlos's demand for a moment. He nodded in agreement, mostly to avoid Bellini's wrath.

Carlos gestured for the workers to leave. They promptly obeyed and hurried outside. Pablo paused at the door, looking back with concern. Carlos caught his stare. "You ain't the only one with experience, old man." Pablo fought his instinct to fight and walked out, joining the others.

Miguel turned to Rigo. "Go take care of it. Don't disappoint me."

Rigo nodded and reluctantly headed out, leaving Carlos surrounded four against one. Miguel eyed the face-down cards on the table.

"Did you lose?" Miguel asked. "You look like a man who loses but don't know it."

"You ain't even seen me play yet."

Miguel picked up Carlos's cards... three Kings. He smirked and walked around the table to reveal the other hands, one at a time.

Carlos tried to keep all four men in his sights. "What the fuck do you want? Where we goin' with this?"

"Don't you mean, 'Where is Rigo going?'"

Carlos's heart raced as he suddenly realized the situation.

"I get that you belong to the angel," Miguel said, flipping cards. "What I can't figure out is why the angel belongs to Brennan. Seems like he's the big winner here." He picked up the final hand of cards - old Pablo's cards - revealing three Aces. "You see? You're a man who loses but just don't know it yet. Just like your piece-of-shit angel."

Carlos snapped and took a swing at Miguel, clocking him in the face, sending him reeling back. He spun around and slammed a second man to the cement floor, stomping his head twice. The two others grabbed Carlos from behind and struggled to restrain him. He quickly broke free with elbows to the ribs. In a blur, the immense guardian kicked the third man in the neck, crushing his throat, and slugged the fourth man in the chest as he reached for his gun, knocking the wind out of him. He followed with a haymaker, striking him hard to a wall. He grabbed him by the hair and shoved his head onto the splintery edge of the table with a sharp crack of bone and an outpouring of blood.

The brutal fight ended with only Carlos and Miguel on their feet. Carlos quickly scanned the floor for the loose gun, but it was knocked away in the brawl.

"Just me and you," Miguel said, catching his breath, reaching into his back pocket. "Better that way."

Miguel jabbed a knife incessantly at Carlos, backing him into a corner until he stabbed him deep in the gut. Carlos slapped the knife away. The two men grappled about the room, knocking over the crude table, falling to the cement floor, the bright Tejano music a stark contrast to the melee.

With Carlos's blood spilling out onto the entangled men, Miguel spotted his associate's gun in a corner. Both men instantly grabbed the weapon. It fired as they struggled for control, the bullet nailing Carlos's lower back. Despite his grave injuries, he soon overpowered Miguel with three head butts against the cement, and pinned him to the floor. With both of them weak, each struggling to grip the gun, Carlos muscled it toward the side of Miguel's neck and pulled the trigger, shooting him point blank, sending a river of blood streaming out the door.

The last two surviving associates rose to their feet in a daze. Still flat on the bloody floor, Carlos held the pistol with both hands and quickly double-tapped them both in the chest, killing them.

Miguel clutched his gaping neck wound. Carlos sat up, gun in hand, and summoned all his strength to shove its barrel to Miguel's forehead. Holding up his palm to shield him from the spatter, Carlos pulled the trigger, ending Miguel's life.

The sounds of violence gone, the Tejano music continued to play joyfully as the pistol tumbled from Carlos's hand. He collapsed near the open door, barely able to move, and glanced at the dark vineyard outside. In his slowed, muddy thoughts, he wondered if he'd see Abel one more time before succumbing to his wound.

* * *

"Let's go, Carlos!" Abel said as he entered the guest house, coming in from the rain. The clouds that had been gathering and darkening all week had finally burst with a downpour that started when Abel began his long trek from the manor. The usual twenty-minute walk became a twelve-minute jog as the trail turned to mud and Abel felt the sting of the cold rain. "Carlos? My arrangement with Bellini is over!"

He'd called out to his friend twice before remembering the poker game, where Carlos was likely having a grand time with the field workers. The sunburnt men not only worked under the intense sun and pressures of harvest all day, but also under the oppression of their bosses always hovering over them. A card game at night in the privacy of their bunkhouse allowed them to relax and be themselves, something Carlos valued and respected.

Abel went into the bedroom and gathered his things into a zippered tote bag - three dress shirts, two pairs of pants, three pairs of socks and underwear - far more than he'd worn in a year as he usually wore the same clothes to the motel each day to match the description Reverend Dean gave to folks he sent his way. He returned to the living room and noticed his friend's duffel bag sitting on the sofa, already packed and ready to go. Abel considered simply waiting for Carlos to have his fill of beer and conversation and return to the guest house, but a clawing feeling urged him to leave the property sooner than later.

He stepped into the kitchen and gathered the rare wines Rosemary had given him. He laid them sideways in the tote bag, admiring the Chardonnay that came especially recommended. As he placed it in the bag with the rest, zipped it shut, and froze upon hearing the tickling of an old piano and the low, passionate voice of Bessie Smith...

*"I've got the blues, I feel so lonely*
*I'll give the world if I could only*
*Make you understand*
*It surely would be grand"*

Abel turned to the living room and stood startled to see Rosemary sitting on the sofa in an alluring black dress. She'd just turned on the stereo, playing the cassette cued to the emotional song, to grab her guest's attention. They looked at each other from across the house with equal desire coupled with opposite intentions - Rosemary determined to seduce, Abel desperate to resist.

*"I'm gonna telephone my baby*
*Ask him won't you please come home*
*'Cause when you're gone*
*I'm worried all day long"*

"You look lovely, Rosemary," Abel said, setting the tote bag of wine onto the dining room table. "I figured you'd be out with David tonight, especially dressed like that."

"I never go out with David," she said, insulted. "The places he frequents aren't meant for wives. They're my old haunts from long ago, but no longer mine to enjoy."

"The mistress that became the wife."

"Don't forget stepmother, a role even less welcome in his dark corners and back-alley clubs. He loves me in his own way, I'm sure, but nothing is less sexy to men like him than the heads of their households." Rosemary picked up Carlos's duffel bag from the sofa and dropped it onto the coffee table, allowing her to stretch out her legs. "Your large friend is at the bunkhouse with the workers."

"Carlos likes to meet new people."

"His kind of people, maybe." She tilted her head and took in the classic blues ballad. "Who's song is this?"

"Bessie Smith, the Empress of the Blues. No voice was more enchanting during the Depression…"

"You know who I mean," Rosemary said with a grin. "I'd love to meet whoever's truly behind this song. I've heard it several times from my room, wandering through the air at night."

*"Baby won't you please come home*
*Baby won't you please come home*
*I have tried in vain*
*Evermore to call your name"*

Abel suddenly felt the presence of his beloved Regina, summoned by their song, undeterred within his heart by the beautiful woman in black lounging on the sofa. Regina sat at the dining table in her white evening gown and spoke to him, their words unheard by their visitor.

"She needs you," Regina said.

"She needs a lot more than me."

"She needs you to help spare her from becoming one of Bellini's gruesome anecdotes. But it's too late for her. You must go."

Abel didn't expect his late wife's grim advice, her gentle soul always encouraging him to help those in need. He noticed a pastel suitcase sitting by the door, Rosemary's last-minute travel case.

"She's walking out on him," Abel said.

"But she doesn't want to walk alone. Leave her be."

He went to the stereo, intent on shutting off the music that now tormented him, but found himself unable to let Regina go, even in such an awkward scene.

Rosemary stood from the sofa and approached Abel at the stereo. She noticed him eyeing her suitcase. "Everything I give a damn about is in there. The rest are gifts for the next trophy wife." She placed her arms around him and whispered in his ear. "Because I follow you, now."

"Is that what you whispered to David? When Eliza and Raymond were still fresh in the ground?"

Rosemary shoved him away, giving up on seducing him.

"You're free to leave anytime, Rosemary, with or without me."

"You know that's not true!"

Abel grabbed his tote bag and Carlos's duffel and headed for the door. Rosemary grabbed his arm, halting him. "David will be gone all night. Right now is the perfect time for us!"

"It's perfect for me and Carlos. I've felt only misery from this place since I arrived. I won't be looking back. Neither should you."

Rosemary laughed. "Carlos. You protect a gorilla thug like that, but you reject me? What makes him so special?"

Abel looked at her in disgust and stepped out into the rain.

# 18

# Unforgivable Things

In the eerie silence of the Devil's Backbone, Abel painfully climbed down the Live Oak tree, tearing his tuxedo on the many jagged branches. He'd watched Regina drift to sleep again and held his panic when he saw her still breathing. After ten agonizing minutes, descending the tree with only one good arm, he landed on the damp ground and made his way to the other car, holding his crucifix tight as he repeated a desperate prayer.

"Please Lord, give me the power to save her. Give me the power to heal. Please Lord, give me the power to save her. Give me the power to heal..."

He found the other car, a demolished lowrider resting at an odd angle against the limestone embankment. Upon reaching the car, he saw four men inside.

The man he'd come to know as Carlos Cruz sat behind the wheel, barely alive, covered in his own blood. His forehead was split, his left shoulder a ripped, mangled mess. Staring straight ahead, the gangster blindly called out to the others.

"Lino... Lino get up... Ozzy... Ignacio... take care of Lino..."

Abel peered into the car. In the front seat beside Carlos sat a man dead from deep lacerations, his head shoved through the windshield. In the back sat another dead man, his neck snapped from the impact, and a teenage boy no older than fifteen, dead from the car's caved roof crushing his body.

Unable to move, unable to even turn his head, Carlos couldn't see his companions, and Abel couldn't bring himself to tell him their fates.

"Lino... stop fuckin' around... Lino..."

Abel saw papers scattered about the car's interior, intricate drawings in graffiti style. He reached for Carlos's hand.

"You okay?" Abel asked. He picked up a drawing and attempted a merciful distraction. "You drew these? These are amazing! Hey, stay with me, Big Man. Talk to me. Did you draw these?" No longer were these men monsters undeserving of pity. Seeing their grisly ends, Abel felt sorrow and shame for condemning them earlier, for telling his wife that he didn't care if they lived or died.

Carlos wheezed, struggling for air in huge gasps. With one final cough of blood, he stopped moving, and his expression froze.

Abel held his crucifix with one hand, Carlos's hand in the other. He shut his eyes and prayed. "Lord, help this man... no pain, no death... let me take it away. Lord, help this man... no pain, no death... let me take it away..."

Gripping Carlos's hand, the sounds and colors of the Devil's Backbone drained and faded as Abel got the feeling for the first time. He absorbed all of Carlos's suffering, healing his massive wounds before his eyes. His mutilated body rebuilt itself, and Abel's eyes widened upon witnessing the incredible sight.

"It's a miracle," Abel said, his voice rising to a crescendo. "A miracle! The Lord has given you new life! THE LORD HAS GIVEN YOU NEW LIFE…"

Abel suddenly bent over and vomited along the side of the car as he released the torment he'd just taken from Carlos. The large gangster sat bolt upright and cried with a strange energy.

"Who are you?" Carlos asked. "I felt it! I felt…" He freed himself from the entanglement of metal and a twisted dashboard, and looked around at his brethren. Seeing their destroyed bodies, his world crashed down around him. He shook them, screamed at them, but knew they were gone. "NO! LINO, NO!"

Abel trembled as he stared at his bloody hands, at the man he just impossibly saved, and quickly realized what he could now do. He looked back at his Corvette up in the Live Oak Tree.

"I felt it, too," Abel said in shock. "I felt it all."

He ran back to Regina.

The rain subsided to a light sprinkle as Abel carried his and Carlos's belongings through the vineyard, up the trail to the field workers' bunkhouse. The extra weight, the chilly night, and the slippery mud made the walk feel twice as long. He'd left Rosemary at the guest house where'd she'd spend the rest of the evening staring at her pastel suitcase, torn between returning to the manor and slinking into bed before David came home, or driving away from Della Luna and into the Bay Area nearly four hours north. The waning moon was partially obscured by clouds, making it hard to see, but the distinct silhouette of the distant bunkhouse served as a beacon.

So dark was the trail that Abel didn't see Rigo standing alone by the vines until he was right in front of him. He'd smelled his cigarette from farther back, but never would have tied the harsh scent to the young man.

"I didn't know you smoked," Abel said. "Coming back from the game?"

Despite their being alone, Rigo stuck to his broken English. "You leave?" Rigo eyed the bags in Abel's hands.

"Word does spread fast around here."

"So is true."

"My work's done. I'm sure we'll see each other again..."

Abel silenced himself when the nervous young man pointed a gun at him, forcing his arm steady. Startled and confused, Abel dropped his bags and raised his hands.

"I am sorry," Rigo said, turning his head to a pair of lights bouncing down the trail toward them. Rather than hide or sheath his pistol, he sidestepped into the vines as if they would conceal him.

"Talk to me, Rigo. What are you doing?"

Before Rigo could recite his rehearsed apology, Livia drove up in the Blue Mule with a case of beer in the passenger seat. She stopped behind Abel, shut off the engine, and stood up in the vehicle with her hands atop the windshield.

"On your way to the game?" she asked them. "Pop's in town, I figured I check it out. Those old guys let me play. They kinda have no choice, if you get me."

With half his body in the vines, Rigo tossed his cigarette to the ground and held his gun at his hip, pointed toward Abel. Livia didn't realize the situation at first, her eyes acclimating from the mule's bright dashboard to the two men standing in the dark. As the scene came into focus, she felt shocked at the sight of the gun, the defeated look on Abel's face, and the forced determination on Rigo's.

"Rigo, what the fuck?" Livia said.

"He tell me," Rigo said in a defiant tone that belied his shaking hand. "He tell me... to do this."

"Put down the fuckin' gun! That Miguel is a turncoat sack of shit!"

"Listen to me, Rigo," Abel said. "You don't have to do what Miguel tells you. We can go to David. We can talk about this."

Rigo cried. He raised his gun at eye level, barely able to keep it steady. "Bellini... he tell me... to do this..."

Livia dropped into her driver's seat, stunned, her arms collapsed onto the steering wheel. Her first instinct was to accuse Rigo of lying, of covering for Miguel, but the lost look on his face told her everything.

Abel slowly lowered his hands, holding his palms out. "Rigo, if you pull that trigger..."

"My bad legs you give back," Rigo said. "I know... but I must..." He rested his finger on the trigger but couldn't bring himself to fire. His face scrunched as his tears turned to a gentle sob.

"I lied," Abel said, "to you, to everyone. I won't give it back, no matter what. But you don't want to do this. I can help you get away."

"Like you help... lady get away? Like you help Brennan sick?"

"What the fuck's he talking about?" Livia asked, confused.

Abel was at a loss for words, seeing that Rigo knew more than he realized. He lowered his arms to his sides. "Then shoot, if you must."

"Whoa, whoa, whoa," Livia said. "Do not fuckin' shoot him!"

Abel held out an outstretched hand, feeling Rigo's burning torment. "David has something on you. You did things for him, unforgivable things you feel you can never return from. So shoot, I won't blame you, and I promise your legs will stay strong. I won't give it back."

Rigo seemed determined to pull the trigger, but fell to his knees in a breakdown. He tossed the gun into the vines and wept into his hands. "I'm sorry... God forgive me..."

Abel grabbed Rigo and threw his arms around him. He held him tight as he let his emotions pour out, crying so hard he couldn't breathe.

During the delicate moment, Livia climbed out of the Mule searched the vines for the gun.

"You have nothing to be sorry about," Abel said. "I know God... God forgives you."

"But Bellini will not."

Rigo pressed his face into Abel's shoulder as they remained embraced. He caught his breath as he remembered...

"Your man... he need you... now..."

Gunshots in the distance made Abel and Livia turn to the bunkhouse ahead. Abel released Rigo and ran down the muddy trail.

Livia quickly returned to the Mule started the engine.

Abel entered the bunkhouse and looked about the room, shocked at the carnage of Carlos, Miguel, and his men sprawled across the bloody floor. He knelt beside his friend and pressed his hands to his chest, healing him within a minute. The rebuilding of Carlos's internal organs and skins felt excruciating at first, almost overwhelming with the unprecedented speed of his divine gift. Carlos gasped for air before breathing normally again, completely spent and gasping for air, but otherwise recovered.

"I thought you was dead, Boss," Carlos said in an exhale, his strength slowly returning.

"Still here, Big Man."

Abel felt a bullet in his hand and hurled it across the room. He scrambled on hands and knees to Miguel's men, but found them all dead. He knelt beside Miguel, cradled his head in his lap, and tried desperately to heal him, moving his hands to different spots on his body to no avail. Abel kept searching for the feeling, shutting his eyes tight as he slid his palms across Miguel's wounds.

"He gave me no choice," Carlos said in an exhale, as he felt his body slowly return to normal.

"I know! But I need to keep..."

"No you don't." Carlos grabbed Abel's arms.

"He never paid me! If he pays me now, then maybe..."

"He don't owe nobody nothin' no more. Let him go."

As Carlos pulled Abel off Miguel's lifeless body, he noticed Livia staring in disbelief from the door. She arrived moments before and witnessed both Carlos's return and Abel's failure to save the others. Carlos saw the helpless confusion in her eyes.

"Boss can't heal the dead."

Twenty-one minutes later, at the front of the manor under a light drizzle, Carlos finished siphoning gas from Miguel's BMW sedan into his lowrider Impala. He gathered the plastic tubing and threw it into his trunk. "All gassed up. Let's get the fuck outta here."

Carlos sat behind the wheel and started the engine. Abel tossed their bags into the backseat and joined his friend. He glanced back at the house and saw Livia standing on the porch.

"Does Brennan own you?" she asked. Abel rolled down his window, startled by her question. "That's why they tried to kill you, yeah? Pop says you work for him in the city. Is it true?"

"I don't work for anyone, not a pastor, not a gangster. No one."

"Bullshit! You worked for my pop!"

"I worked for your mother and the field workers, and now I'm leaving."

"Does Brennan own you?" Livia said, screaming. "I want the truth!"

BLAM!

Livia fired a gun into the air, the pistol Rigo had tossed into the vines in shame. The gunshot rang across the property, scattering a flock of nesting birds from a nearby tree. Abel stared, mesmerized by the sight.

"I think you know the truth about me, Livia. And I think you know the truth about everyone else."

Livia lowered her gun, unsure about anything. Abel rolled up his window and nodded to Carlos to drive away, leaving the young girl alone on the porch.

She stood in silence, frozen for ten minutes, wondering about everything she'd seen and everything she knew about her father.

Muttering a curse, she pocketed her gun, got into her pickup truck, and started the engine.

# 19

# Into the Stars

Abel's lungs were ready to explode when he returned to Regina's tree. He ran down the ravine from Carlos's lowrider upended on a limestone embankment to his wrecked Corvette trapped high in an ancient Live Oak. He stumbled in the dark, falling to the shallow mud several times, his balance off because of his immobile right arm. Bessie Smith's eternal crooning greeted him along a soft breeze, a tranquil night scene that belied the urgency and peril. Abel realized the classic blues single would repeat in a loop until the car's battery ran dry. It felt like a ticking clock, as if Regina would cling to life so long as Bessie sang, both women to fade out along with the final notes on the old piano.

Looking for a good handhold for his torturous climb, he spotted an injured bird, barely alive at the base of the tree.

He saw at least a dozen more, failing in the mud, a flock of Starlings that had been nesting in the tree during the crash. On pure instinct, Abel placed his left hand on the struggling bird and felt a strange, frightening sensation run through him, the crack and burn of tiny snapped bones.

The little bird fluttered its wings under his palm, and he could barely breathe in excitement as it flew into the sky. He crouched down and gently touched the many other birds around him with both hands, reversing their injuries and sending them off into the night.

Abel gasped in disbelief, a bright smile spanning his face as he gazed at his hands. He touched the last three birds, but they remained unmoving, dead from the impact of the crash.

Emerging from his lowrider, Carlos watched from afar. He saw the kind stranger crouched in the mud over the small flock, the little birds fluttering away upon his touch, and instantly knew what he was witnessing. The Black man in the tuxedo and busted glasses had a divine gift, one that he shared with Carlos but not the deserving men he saw as his brothers. He blamed not God nor Abel for his loss. The power he felt from that holy union told him poor timing alone resulted in his tragedy. He wondered if his savior would agree.

Abel climbed the tree and soon reached his car to find Regina still asleep inside. Because of the odd angle and his injured right arm, he could only reach toward her with his left, a painful effort that burned as he stretched in through the busted passenger window. Her closed eyes and blank expression doused his flicker of hope as his fingers finally held hers.

"Baby, you still with me? You gotta be here with me! I called for help. They just gotta find us!" Regina didn't respond. As they barely held hands, his fingers sliding on her satin glove, Abel feared the worst. His comforting words turned to desperate cries. "And I prayed, Love! I prayed to the Lord and He answered! I asked for His gift and He gave it! You need to see for yourself!"

Regina slowly opened her eyes, the only part of her body that could still move. Abel felt a wave of relief. "Good! You can't doze off now! I did what you said, I found the other driver. And God healed him, Regina! He healed him through me!"

Regina could only stare blankly at her husband.

"The poor guy was ripped apart. I touched his hand and right away I felt his pain pour into me like sand through an hourglass. Then it was done, all the pain drained out. Made me sick as Hell but he'll live! And so will you!"

He gripped her hand tight. Her frozen gaze allowed a single tear.

"And I healed birds! A flock of Starlings! They must have been asleep in the tree when we... they were dying on the ground, Regina. But I took away their pain! I placed my hand on them and they flew, Regina! They flew up into the stars!"

A trace of a smile crept onto Regina's stone face. "You did good, baby," she whispered in a breath. "You keep doing good." Bessie Smith continued to lament her blues, begging her man to come home, as Regina shut her eyes one last time.

Abel flew into a panic. He grunted as he painfully stretched himself further into the car, grabbing a firm hold of her hand, her arm, searching for a feeling that would never come.

"Lord NO!" Abel screamed, looking about the tree's dense foliage and thick branches as if the mighty Live Oak that held them was God Himself. "Please, Lord! Don't do this! Don't take her from me! NO! REGINA!" He couldn't fathom why his new power had failed him, his mind spinning when the realization struck him like a cold splash...

She wore long satin gloves.

Abel peeled off her glove and squeezed her hand tight, the warmth of her skin offering a moment of false hope. He wiggled himself deeper into the car and was confronted by the grisly sight of the lower half of her body, crushed nearly flat against the dashboard. He embraced her lifeless body with both arms, his sorrow turning to seething rage. As he held his wife's head to his chest, he let out a furious, gut-wrenching scream.

At the base of the tree, as Carlos heard the man howl in agony, he knew he was witnessing their final moment together, realizing the tragedy of his savior's sacrifice.

"What have I done?" Carlos said, muttering in Spanish.

Abel's screams echoed across the ravine, a sound both piercing and primal. In that cruel moment, Abel had gone mad.

"Why weren't you there with her?" Abel shouted to the sky. "Tell me! WHY WEREN'T YOU THERE?"

"He'll be there," Abel said as he checked his phone's texts again. He scrolled up and down, searching for any kind of response to his urgent message.

"I don't think so," Carlos said, driving them back to the city. "The reverend's asleep. Lucky him." The rural highway stretched mostly empty at that time of night, allowing him to push his old engine to its limit.

Abel sent another frantic text, his twentieth in as many minutes. Carlos tried to slap his phone away.

"Boss, don't let that dumb-ass girl get to you. Forget what she said about Brennan and Bellini, she don't know shit. Put your phone away."

"She's telling the truth. I need to keep trying. I need to reach the reverend right away."

"Why now? Why not in the morning?"

"We won't be here in the morning," Abel said, dropping the sudden news. "If we're lucky, we'll be three-hundred miles away before the sun comes up."

Carlos cursed, slamming his fists to the steering wheel in frustration. "This is bullshit, Boss! That fuckin' mess back there was all Miguel! That prick had it out for us from the beginning! He couldn't stand you gettin' the respect he wanted! That's all!"

"That may be, Carlos, but it's not just Livia. Rigo said pretty much the same thing. If they're right, and Bellini thinks we're working for his rival, we need to hit the road away from La Fig. Remember the last time powerful men fought over me?"

"Remember phone calls? Just dial him up! Make the call!"

David Bellini made a phone call from the back of his limousine on his way to Santa Maria for an overnight stay at one of those decadent, shadowy places where wives aren't welcome. He looked out the window at the Central Coast coming into view and thought about the events he'd put into motion before leaving Della Luna. Though he trusted his men, it occurred to him they'd never dealt with someone like Abel before.

On that thought, he pulled out his phone and made a call.

"Is it done? Are we... get a hold of yourself... calm down... I said calm down... just answer my question... hold on... what about Miguel?" The desperate voice on the other end detailed the evening. David leaned forward and grabbed his driver's shoulder. "Turn back! Now!"

Twenty-six minutes later, David's limo returned to the manor and parked in front of the grand house. The driver stepped out, walked around to open David's door, but his impatient employer had already gotten out and headed for the front house.

Rigo stood on the porch, nervously puffing a cigarette, looking down at the ten snuffed smokes at his feet. David approached him, barely containing his anger.

"I gave you a simple task," David said, "one that you've performed for me many times. Your failure is a betrayal."

Rigo looked at his feet in shame. David held Rigo's face, forcing him to respond eye-to-eye.

"He is.. the hand of God!" Rigo said, fighting his fears.

"You owe it to me, Rodrigo! And now you owe it to Miguel! To his men!" Rigo stared at his boss with empty eyes. David calmed himself, chose his words with precision. "You owe it to Emilia and Luciana."

Rigo snapped out of his daze with a look of worry. "I didn't betray you..."

"But you did, Rigo." David spoke slowly, his eyes fixed on his trustee. "I now need to replace poor Miguel. That means I may have to pull the men protecting Emilia and Luciana. Think of what Brennan will do when they're alone. You betrayed me, them, and you betrayed him, Rodrigo, when you came here, or don't you remember?"

"I remember," Rigo said, muttering to himself. He looked away as he cried. David shifted his business tone to one of comfort and compassion.

"I understand, Rodrigo. You feared Grant would make you a cripple again. That's his real power. He's a loan shark with your soul. But make things right, do what I ask, and all is forgiven. I'll move your mother and sister to Della Luna. The guest house will be theirs where they'll be safe for the rest of their lives. Even the 'Hand of God' can't offer you that. You follow me, son?"

Rigo wiped away his tears and looked his boss in the eye, considering the weight of his gentle command.

"I follow you, boss."

# 20

## Deal With The Devil

The rain pounded the spire of St. Nelia's Church, dark and seemingly empty in the wee hours of the night, its iron cross swaying in the wind of an approaching storm. Dark clouds had opened to a downpour as Abel and Carlos drove into La Figueira's city limits twenty minutes before. The heavy rain seemed to follow them down Arrowhead Avenue, turning onto H Street, and turning again onto the property of the inner-city church.

Carlos drove over a curb and parked as close as he could to the church entrance to minimize Abel's exposure to the cold rain. He shut off the engine, allowing the sound of the aggressive patter on the Impala's roof to fill the cabin. He turned to his boss with one last plea he knew would land on deaf ears.

"Call the reverend from the road," Carlos said, "when we're two states away. Should I beg?"

"I did that before, with Goldie, left him holding the bag. I was a coward."

"You was a survivor. If we didn't take off from Texas the way we did, we'd probably be dead and buried out in the desert near Marfa. They'd turn your grave into an art piece, a tourist spot that gives you good luck."

"You don't know that."

"Maybe not, but I know for sure that all the folks you helped here in La Fig these past few years would be dead by now if we hadn't showed up. Same with all the towns along the way."

"Go home, Carlos." Abel's cell phone dinged. He nodded as he read a text message, much to Carlos's dismay.

"He is still here, ain't he?" Carlos asked.

"He waited. I knew he would."

Carlos looked around the seemingly vacant parking lot. "Boss, I don't like this..."

"I live only three blocks away. Don't worry about me, Big Man. Just go home, pack your bags, wipe the place clean, say your goodbyes..."

"Ain't no goodbyes to make."

"Then just meet me at my place in forty-five minutes."

Before Carlos could protest further, Abel opened his door and stepped out into the relentless rain. He jogged to the church entrance, pausing under the eave of the portal to give his friend one last wave. He shouted "forty-five minutes" before heading inside.

Carlos started his car and drove back to the motel to collect his things and remove any evidence of their extended stay. As he navigated the flooded streets, he realized he was wrong, that he had goodbyes ahead of him after all. Three families had been living in their cars in a field a few blocks down Arrowhead. To protect Abel's identity, Carlos had always kept them and everyone else away from the motel. Now that he and Abel were leaving the city, he would bang on their windshields during a storm, waking them in the dead of night, and give them the keys to the fifteen rooms of the Royal Queen where they'd be greeted by blankets, pillows, doors with working locks, and an office full of donated baked goods. If they asked him for assistance moving into the old building, ensuring that the rooms were truly vacant, he'd help them, for that's what Abel would want.

It would unfortunately take more than forty-five minutes.

Abel entered the church's dark chapel, candles lighting only its pulpit. He saw Reverend Dean kneeling behind it, staring up at Jesus on the cross in silent prayer. Abel approached his friend who sensed his arrival yet remained on his knees, his eyes fixed on the holy symbol.

"Thank you for meeting me, Reverend."

"It's no problem. I was here late anyway." Abel knelt beside him. "Joining me in prayer?"

"Maybe. I still talk to Him once in a while, if only to yell at Him. Will you hear my latest sins?"

"Always."

"I'm afraid I made a deal with a devil," Abel said. "I'm afraid people will be hurt if I remain. Carlos and I are leaving the city tonight."

"You do what you must."

Abel didn't expect such immediate acceptance of his decision to leave. "I wanted... needed... to tell you in person. I want to thank you for helping me over the past few years. You've done your congregation a great service, but it's time I go."

"We figured as much."

"We?"

Reverend Dean continued to stare at the cross. "Arlo helped me piece together what you're going through. He reminded me that every man wrestles with temptation, particularly those who are angry with The Lord."

"What are you getting at, Reverend?"

"Carlos told me about Texas, about the men who paid a fortune for your gift. The war they waged over you. The men - the children - who fell in the crossfire. I understand it's hard to turn them down. I know it's why you ran. You took their blood money and left town. And now you're doing it again."

Abel stood and looked at the reverend, still kneeling at the cross, as if he had lost his mind. "I'm not taking anything. I forwarded you the money. For the church. For you."

"That transaction was cancelled earlier today. And now you're here, giving me your guilty goodbye. Is that how it went that last night in Texas? Or did you just drive away?"

"Exactly who have you been talking to?"

Reverend Dean turned slightly to face his old friend for the first time. "I'll still pray for you, Abel. I'm sad to say it's all I can do now."

Abel had often considered telling him everything - the details of Regina's death, Pastor Goldie Reeves's elaborate grift, and Bellini's unstable crew - but feared damaging their friendship, splintering the delicate trust between them. He felt ashamed of his work with Pastor Goldie, his early attempt to cash in on his gift in a misguided defiance against The Lord. He didn't want a good man like Dean to see him in the same light as those con artists touring the revival circuit, adorned in white suits, gold jewelry, and false promises.

"Reverend, please understand..."

"He understands just fine," a man's voice said, echoing across the chapel.

Startled and alarmed, Abel recognized the voice. He turned to see Brennan and Mr. Felix step out from the darkness. "Mr. Brennan. I didn't see your fancy sports car out front."

"Parked it in the back," Brennan said, "under a canopy next to my Sunday school." The two men approached the pulpit but kept their distance. "What was it you said? 'I'm afraid I made a deal with a devil.' That sure as hell sounds like Bellini, right Mr. Felix?"

Felix nodded, his hands in his coat pockets. Abel suddenly felt nervous. He looked down at his friend still kneeling, his eyes shut as if to block out the evil men around him.

"Well, now you're gonna make a deal with this devil," Brennan said. "And when you're done, and I get my life back, you can leave with your thug bodyguard and move far away into some other ghetto until you can fleece another rich sucker. Unlike Bellini, I ain't trying to own you like a dog."

"You men have it all wrong," Abel said, silencing himself as Mr. Felix pointed a gun at him.

"Heal me, Mr. Grant. Or is it 'Brother Rapha'? I guess you change your name every time you change your business address."

Abel took a last look at Reverend Dean, who offered no solace. He turned to face Brennan and his associate's gun. "I fear losing my friend's respect, his back turned to me, and I fear you may be lost to reason. But I do not fear death. You know that."

"Yeah. I know." Brennan nodded to Felix, who swung his pistol at the reverend. "But everyone's afraid of something. Even Black angels."

Another man with a gun raised stepped out of shadow and into the soft candlelight, and for a moment Abel feared it was another of Brennan's enforcers flanking him.

"Put it down!" Arlo said, his commanding voice seizing the room. He pointed his gun at Mr. Felix from across the chapel.

"You're not supposed to be here," Brennan said.

"Yeah, but I had a naggin' feeling to come back."

"Walk away, Mr. Arlo. Leave me to take care of business."

The large roughneck had fire in his eyes, enraged by the sight of Mr. Felix still aiming his weapon at the reverend. "This wasn't what we talked about!"

"As I recall, you did all the talking. Now the talking is done.'

"I said put it down!"

Brennan revealed his own gun and pointed it at Arlo, whose rage was unabated. "Walk away before you're no longer able to."

"I ain't exactly afraid to die either! Put it down! Now!"

The men held their weapons tight in a three-way standoff, with Abel caught in the middle. "Gentlemen, there's no need for violence."

"Look at us!" Brennan said. "A bunch of brave fools! The Grim Reaper awaits! But I'm the only one here who's been knocking on his door. Mr. Felix, please..."

Abel saw his worst fears unfold in an instant...

Mr. Felix shot Reverend Dean in the back. Arlo shot Felix in the chest, sending him dead to the pews. Brennan shot Arlo in the gut, felling him where he stood. Arlo collapsed to the floor, swung his gun around, and plugged Brennan in the head.

Abel rushed to Reverend Dean and slapped his palms onto his back. He felt the pain of his friend's wound surge into him as the grisly gunshot repaired itself.

Abel scrambled to Arlo and pressed his hands to the man's stomach. Still sick and spent from so quickly healing Dean, Abel struggled to find that feeling.

"Save him!" Reverend Dean yelled, gasping for air as if emerging from a drowning death.

Abel shifted his grip, trying desperately to heal Arlo, but knew he'd gotten to him a few seconds too late. Willing his divine power to arise, he passed out atop Arlo's body.

Reverend Dean crawled to Abel and failed to wake him. He ran to the holy water font at the back of the chapel and soaked his robe, returning to squeeze the blessed water onto

Abel's face. Slowly, he opened his eyes, groggy from his stupor.

"Just breathe, son," Reverend Dean said. "You must live. Breathe now."

"I'm sorry... couldn't save them." Abel struggled to speak. He'd arrived at the church still weak from healing Carlos, but now felt a new level of torment from quickly saving the reverend and attempting to revive Arlo. Never had he used his gift so intensely, in moments so close together.

"Be silent. We can't save them all."

"I wasn't in this for the money," Abel said, his voice hoarse and wheezing. "I kept my past... out of shame..."

"I understand, but you must breathe. Get to your feet. Pastor Samuel is in the school. He heard the gunshots and likely picked up the phone. The police will be here soon." He helped Abel stand but was hesitate to release him, his legs ready to buckle.

"The money..." Abel moaned.

"This church is done taking money from men like Brennan, men like Bellini. We don't work for them."

"You must understand..."

"I forgive you. Now go!" Reverend Dean checked the time on his watch and looked at the double doors as if a swat team would burst in at any moment. He helped Abel outside to the dense rain. With one last embrace, he backed away and watched his friend stagger out to the flooded street.

# 21

# Give and Take

Abel limped down flooded alleys and cut across abandoned lots, making his way back to H Street, back to the North Star Arms. Along the way, he clung to brick walls and chain-link fences, grabbed hold of trash cans, and reached out for telephone poles. Drained and disoriented, he used every object in his path to feel his way through the dark and dense rain, and to help keep him on his feet.

Every moment felt like the verge of total collapse, every step a conscious effort to keep moving forward. The one thought that drove him was to get out of town before more people got hurt or killed. He kept hearing Reverend Dean's sermon, its closing line repeating in his head: "You share the scars of those you wound." To Abel, there were no truer words, for his body felt adorned head-to-heels with the scars of both the wicked and the weary, of powerful men whose ignorance and greed left burning trails of pain and suffering in their wakes. In the Dallas-Fort Worth area of Texas, in the Greater La Figueira region of California, and in the many small towns in between he'd visited, Abel met those in Need and those in Want, the latter always emboldened by undeserved entitlement stemming from their wealth and power and privilege.

Upon reaching H Street, Abel stood startled by how foreboding his neighborhood seemed. The late hour coupled with his foggy state gave his street a liminal sense, a quiet desolation even he was unaccustomed to. The gangsters, hustlers, and homeless were all asleep, though it felt as if they'd been erased from the world.

Walking up the stone stairs to his building's door, Abel wished he could see Marci's face smiling down at him from the top step one last time. Surely, she was asleep in her apartment - maybe alone, maybe not - but she may as well have been spirited away to another life. With Carlos on route and the highway calling, Abel felt a wave of sadness upon realizing that he'd likely never see Marci Williams again. Though he resented telling anyone what to do, he often thought about indirectly helping the community rebuild their lives the way Reverend Dean did, of guiding Marci away from the life of a sex worker and into something more fulfilling and dignified. He recalled that she'd always loved animals.

None of that would happen now. Marci would stand at the top of the steps the following evening and wonder where her friend the "handyman" had vanished to. A week later, she'd conclude that Abel had moved on, another supposed friend come and gone with no forwarding address or phone. His sudden absence would further support her pessimistic view of life, that she couldn't depend on anyone, that she wasn't meant to experience a stable relationship. In his delirium, his whirlwind of regret and sorrow, pangs of guilt stabbed at him with each step toward her usual spot above. Despite her fierce independence, he felt responsible for her.

Abel climbed the stairs of the North Star Arms, one excruciating step at a time, with more stairs awaiting inside.

* * *

Abel entered his apartment, its busted door still ajar even though it now had a working knob. He gathered a few of his belongings - his clothes, records, photo albums, and other small mementos - and piled them together on the small desk he would leave behind for the next tenant. He saved his treasured turntable for last, with Bessie Smith cued and still ready to sing. Rather than unplug and pack up the antique machine, he switched it on, starting the old blues record. The piano melody immediately calmed him as "Baby Won't You Please Come Home" played in that studio for the last time.

Regina appeared, her body a blur in the center of the room. As always, Abel couldn't see his late wife, but felt her standing before him.

"Tough time again, baby," she said. "A lot of bad men want a piece of you."

"Same old story wherever I go," Abel said, realizing he was actually speaking with his wiser inner self. He sat on the couch for his first moment of rest all day. "I was a coward before, and I'm an idiot now. More folks died because of me, because of my poor judgement. Please, Regina, tell me what to do."

Regina walked up to her husband and looked in his eyes. He felt her warm touch on his cheek, heard her voice and felt her breath as she spoke, and in that beautiful moment he allowed himself to believe that perhaps he wasn't alone. Perhaps his late wife truly watched over him, summoned by their song. He barely had the strength to sit upright as he watched the floorboards glow with her every footstep when she walked to the door and turned with an unexpected final word.

"Run."

Abel looked up at his wife and was startled to see David and Rigo standing in her place at the open doorway, Rigo's pistol raised and pointed at him.

BLAM!

Abel felt the bullet lodge into his stomach. He slid off the couch, onto his side on the hardwood floor. He clutched his wound in shock, barely hanging on.

"Forgive me," Rigo said, tears streaming down his face. He glanced back at his boss in the hall before adjusting the gun, aiming it at Abel's head.

Abel's vision faded. He could barely make out the two men across the room, but felt Rigo's pain, his torture over choosing between family and the man who renewed both his health and his faith. As Abel's life hung over him, he felt only pity for his would-be killer.

"Finish it, Rigo," David said.

"You have your reasons, Rigo," Abel said. "Do as the man says... finish it... it's alright... it's over now..."

Rigo held his gun with both hands, the weapon feeling heavy and hot. He trembled, crying in fury and anger as he tried to pump himself up for the unimaginable deed that must be done. His sister and mother filled his thoughts, but no longer motivated his actions. Instead, he felt them urging him to do the right thing.

He lowered his gun and wept at seeing the angel's blood patter to the floor, each drop a sin for which he'd never be redeemed. "I am sorry."

"Go ahead, Rigo," Abel said. "I'm ready."

The young man aimed his gun again, resting his finger on the trigger, but couldn't bring himself to pull it.

"That's enough, son," David said, calmly placing his hand on the pistol. He took it from his trustee who seemed eager to part with it.

BLAM!

Rigo fell dead to the floor, his left temple spurting blood.

Abel looked past Rigo's body to David, smoking gun in hand. "You bastard!" He stared at David with venom as he stepped across the threshold and into the studio apartment, standing over his fallen trustee.

"It had to be done, Mr. Grant." David knelt beside Rigo with genuine sorrow. "I tried. I gave the boy a second chance, then a third, but even with his family at stake, even with you begging him to pull the trigger... Now I know I could never fully trust him again, and trust in the one thing we have in this world."

"To Hell with your world!" The room spun, its lights dimming, as Abel tried to keep focus on David. "Bellini... you'll pay for this... Carlos..."

"Carlos, yes," David said, lowering his gun. "I'm surprised he's not here, which means he'll be here any minute so you can fly off to another city. I appreciate your concern, but I can handle any man coming, even your mighty guardian."

Abel wheezed, gasping for breath, as he pushed off the floor and propped himself up on his elbows. Even faced with David's atrocity, he felt the need to warn him. "Bellini... you don't understand... even I wouldn't be able to stop him... he won't just kill you... he will burn everything you love to the ground... he'll never stop, and you won't see him coming."

"I make it a point to see everything coming, and I know all about Carlos Cruz. A legend, a one-man army. It's no wonder you brainwashed him into becoming your disciple. Bravo, Mr. Grant."

"You don't... understand."

"I understand all too well."

"Then finish it... if you must."

"That's just it," David said. "I don't think I must. No, you're already on your way out. Best we enjoy each other's company in your final minutes."

"You're... a sick man..."

Bessie Smith continued to sing her soulful ballad as David watched Abel dying on the floor. Regina sat beside him, and in that desperate moment he saw her angelic face for the first time in a decade, their reunion soon to come.

"'The Lord giveth and The Lord taketh away,'" David said. "That's what you told me when you healed Rosemary, when you took away her cancer. But I had no idea that you were literally taking her away from me, that you were working for my enemies. Even I play the fool sometimes."

Abel struggled to rise to his feet, defying Death's pull. David grinned as Abel stumbled across the room toward him, awkwardly lunging at him and grabbing his gun with no strength to speak of. In a sudden desperate rush, Abel somehow knocked the gun across the floor and into the hall. David struck him in the face, sending him down to his knees.

David turned to the hallway in time to see Livia pick up the loose gun in her left hand, Rigo's old gun in her right. Frightened, torn, she awkwardly pointed both at her father.

"Livia, give me them to me."

"No! You're gonna kill me, too! You can't fully, completely trust me now. And trust is all we got, yeah?"

"Don't be foolish. Give them to me."

"I was foolish, Pop, you got that right. I know you killed my mother. Raymond. Rigo. Abel. You killed a lot of people. But I told myself it couldn't be true. Foolish me."

"Don't do it," Abel said in a mutter. "Livia..."

"Why the hell not?"

"There are... two kinds of people. You choose... which kind you are."

"More poetry," David said. "Even now."

Livia held the guns tight as her father approached her, extending his hands. He gently took both guns from her. Disarmed and on the verge of tears, Livia looked up at her father, expecting a scolding or a dose of tough love. Instead, David pistol whipped Livia and shoved her down to the floor. He pocketed Rigo's gun and shook his head in regret.

"We're all fools here, Livia," David said. He stamped down his hesitation, seeing it as a weak sentiment. "You, your tramp mother, her gigolo mechanic, the dying angel. Don't you see I have no choice! I can't afford to be anyone's fool! But now you've cornered me, my own blood, and I don't know what to do with you." David looked down at Rigo's lifeless body and at Abel bleeding out on the floor before turning back to his daughter, his gun heavy and searing in his grip. Forcing away second thoughts, punching down his nagging conscience, he pointed it at her.

"Pop? What the hell?" Livia's voice wavered as she bumped against a wall while backing away. "You need help!"

"We all do," David said down the barrel of the gun, fighting back tears. "Perhaps I'll see you roaming the halls. Perhaps, in time, I'll forget you were ever there. Either way, as Grant said, I'm ready."

"Pop, please..."

Regina knelt in front of Abel and cradled his face in her hands, his fear palpable, overwhelming. "Don't be afraid of death, Baby."

"I don't fear my own."

"Yours, hers, mine, you need to accept that death is not the end. How could it be that simple? She's on her path and you're on yours. Reverend said you can't save them all. Come with me now. You knew we'd be together again one day." She extended her hand.

Barely breathing, curled on the floor, Abel looked up his wife, saw the light shining in her eyes. "One day."

Bessie Smith's song ended, resetting the turntable, throwing the room into silence. Regina faded away, revealing the frightened young girl near the door.

Abel hurled himself forward and grabbed David's leg, making him instantly collapse as if his life were draining away.

"What are you doing?" David asked in a panic.

"The Lord giveth, The Lord taketh... and The Lord giveth again..."

Blood streamed from all over David's body as Abel gave him all the disease and pain he took from so many others. David's legs snapped at the knees, and his neck and face burst with bloody tumors. Livia could only watch in shock at the gory sight of her father writhing in agony. Within moments, David lay dead.

Livia cried out in a long, suffering moan, but didn't run to her father. She stood motionless, staring down at his mutilated body. In that pivotal moment, she knew her cries were not for his death but for his final truth.

"I think I always knew," Livia said. "I always knew we wasn't family. We was just things in his life, like his car or his clothes or his land. I always knew."

Seeing the two men side-by-side on the floor, she chose to kneel beside Abel as he clung to life. He'd spent what little of time left toward saving hers. As he shut his eyes, she took his hand.

"All the people you saved," she said, "all the families you helped, and here you lay dying in this cesspit of a city. Is this really God's way? I wish you could heal yourself. I wish I could heal you."

*Lynn Harrod*

Abel clutched her hand and pressed it to his wound. She stirred, looked around the room, overwhelmed as she experienced the feeling.

His wound healed before her eyes, the bullet falling from his gut, plunking onto the hardwood floor. His tired breathing grew into gasps as he opened his eyes wide, looking up at the girl.

"You did it," Livia said in wonder. "You can heal yourself."

"No, I can't." Abel smiled and shook his head, something Livia didn't understand. As she helped him sit up, Carlos entered, stunned at the carnage. He looked at Rigo's shattered temple and at the grisly sight of David's mutilated corpse.

"Shit, Boss! What the fuck happened?"

"Tell me while you're at it," Livia said.

Abel took a moment to breathe. "The difference between an angel and a demon, the two kinds of people, is just give and take. All the pain, all the suffering that I've taken from so many... I gave it all to your father." He looked into Livia's eyes. "The rest I gave to you."

Livia looked at her hands, then looked at Abel. She shook from the realization and dry heaved in pain, spewing forth all the torment he absorbed all evening, now pouring out through her.

"I wish I could say you'll get used to that," Abel said. "But you won't."

Abel rose to his feet, groggy but alive and on the mend. He picked up his bag and joined Carlos by the door. Livia remained on her knees, frozen in shock, still trying to comprehend what had just happened.

"Where are you going?" she asked.

"You won't need me anymore. You're the angel now. Goodbye, Livia."

Still weak, barely able to stand, Carlos helped him to the door and out into the hall. Livia stared at her trembling hands as if for the first time. She looked down at her father's body and quietly wept for the man he used to be.

# 22

# Final Lesson

The morning sun streamed through the dirty windows, through the gaps in the aluminum foil that partially covered the glass. Abel opened his eyes to the light, waking from his first blissful sleep in ages. The lumpy bed, stained walls, and overflowing ashtray on the bedside table told him he was back in Room 9 of the abandoned Royal Queen Motel. He sat up, sore, tired, but otherwise himself again.

Carlos sat on a chair at the foot of the bed, also waking up from another long, anxious night.

"Why are we back here?" Abel asked.

"You weren't in no shape to hit the road. Never seen you like that. For reals, I wasn't sure you'd make it."

"How long?"

"You slept a whole fuckin' day. I almost called a doctor. But you good now, right? How you feel?"

"I feel like... weeds pulled from a garden."

Abel reached into his tote bag and pulled out a pack of White Knights. He slammed the pack in his palm, slid out a cigarette, and flicked on his lighter, only to gaze at its tall flame in astonishment. He put the lighter back in his bag and tossed the pack into the trash can by the nightstand. Abel saw Carlos looking at him, curious.

"Nothing," Abel said.

"What's that mean?" Carlos asked. "Nothing?"

"It means exactly that. For the first time in years, that's what I feel. Nothing. I don't feel the urge to smoke to numb the pain from everyone around me. I don't feel the pinched nerve in your lower back, the rumble in your stomach, or the desperation of the squatters nearby. And I don't feel Regina waiting for me to play her song. I feel nothing at all. I'm an empty vessel."

Carlos's eyes widened upon realizing what his boss was saying. "Damn, so it's true? What's the girl gonna do with it now?"

"You'd have to ask her. All I can say is may God have mercy on her. She'll need it." Abel stood and picked up his tote bag. "Let's find a new town."

"But you can't... I mean... you lost your... you know."

"You don't need to be 'God's Hand' to help people, Carlos. That may very well be His final lesson for me. It's wisdom that's worth more than all the bibles and all the churches in the world."

"So, you're hearing Him, now?"

"I've always heard Him, Big Man. But now, I'm listening."
Abel headed for the door, but Carlos stopped him.

"Boss, you got a visitor."

* * *

Abel and Carlos emerged from Room 9 to see Marci sitting on
the front bumper of the lowrider. She ran to Abel as he
stepped out onto the lot.

"I heard gunshots," Marci said, "but I was scared. I stayed
inside, called the cops, but you know they don't exactly rush
to our neighborhood..."

"It's alright, Marci. I'm alright."

"So it's true, everything I heard. You're the angel."

"Not anymore."

Abel touched her face, turning it to find fresh bruises
across her left cheek. She pulled his hand away.

"Goes with the profession," she said.

"So get a new profession. I am."

Carlos sat behind the wheel of his Impala and started the
engine.

"You take care of him," Marci said, peering into the car at
Carlos. She turned to Abel as he joined his friend in the front
seat. "You make sure your scary gangster watches over you."

"He may be scary, may be hard to understand, but I know
the truth. He's always watching over me."

Carlos shifted into gear and drove them away, out of the lot
and onto Arrowhead Avenue. Instead of turning left, heading

west and deeper into the city, they turned right to drive east, away from La Figueira and the St. Nelia District.

Marci stood alone in the motel lot and watched the lowrider leave the city limits. She walked down the corridor, past the rooms filled with homeless families, squatters, and vagrants. Upon reaching Carlos's old office, she caught sight of her reflection in the walk-up window.

Her bruises were gone.

*Lynn Harrod*

Lionheart Park Retirement Village offers its residents a luxurious resort setting with quaint cottages by the sea. Within this paradise is a profound sorrow, a need to feel loved again. Eloise spends her time in the garden caring for the flowers and statues. Her lonely routine takes a turn when she finds a wounded crow that changes the everyone's lives. Family can be found in the unlikeliest of places in this novella by veteran writer Lynn Harrod.

**Keepers of the Night Garden**
Available on
www.deerwoodpress.com

# About the Author

Lynn Harrod is an award-winning writer, artist, filmmaker, and educator with over 30 years of experience crafting shorts, essays, and screenplays. His characters often find their worlds spun sideways by a startling revelation.

Lynn was awarded the PRSA Image Award of Excellence and has placed in the Quarterfinals and Semifinals of the Nicholl Fellowship, the Finals of the Nevada Film Office Competition, the Semifinals of the Writers' Network Competition, and twice in the Semifinals of the FadeIn Awards.

Born in Texas, raised in California's San Joaquin Valley, educated and trained in Hollywood, Lynn is a writer and partner with Only Human Productions, where several of his works are in development. When he's not spending time with his wife and daughter, or writing all night on his patio, he's usually having a pint with friends.